W9-BAY-770

Also by Anne-Laure Bondoux

Life As It Comes
The Killer's Tears
The Destiny of Linus Hoppe
The Second Life of Linus Hoppe

anne-laure bondoux

LEADER OF THE TRIBE

Translated from the French by Y. Maudet

delacorte press

Published by Delacorte Press
an imprint of Random House Children's Books
a division of Random House, Inc.
New York

This is a work of fiction. Names, characters, places, and incidents either are the
product of the author's imagination or are used fictitiously. Any resemblance to
actual persons, living or dead, events, or locales is entirely coincidental.

Text copyright © 2004 by Bayard Editions Jeunesse
Translation copyright © 2007 by Y. Maudet
Jacket illustration copyright © 2007 by Dan Craig

Originally published in France in 2004 by Bayard Editions Jeunesse
under the title *La Tribu*.

All rights reserved.

Delacorte Press and colophon are registered trademarks of Random House, Inc.

www.randomhouse.com/kids

Educators and librarians, for a variety of teaching tools, visit us at
www.randomhouse.com/teachers

Library of Congress Cataloging-in-Publication Data
Bondoux, Anne-Laure.
[Tribu. English]
Vasco, leader of the tribe / Anne-Laure Bondoux ; translated from the French
by Y. Maudet. — 1st ed.
p. cm.
Summary: Following his dreams of finding a safe haven in a new place, Vasco leads a
motley group of rats out of the city, through a dangerous sea voyage, and finally to a
forest where the rats, now a true tribe, can make a fresh start.
ISBN 978-0-385-73363-2 (trade) — ISBN 978-0-385-90378-3 (lib. bdg.)
[1. Survival—Fiction. 2. Rats—Fiction. 3. Voyages and travels—Fiction.
4. Toleration—Fiction.] I. Maudet, Y. II. Title.
PZ7.B63696Vas 2007
[Fic]—dc22
2006101155

The text of this book is set in 12-point Goudy.

Printed in the United States of America

10 9 8 7 6 5 4 3 2 1

First American Edition

This story was imagined with the invaluable input of
Patrick Bideault and Thomas Leclere.
Thanks to them.

Contents

PART 1—UNDER THREAT

PART 2—IN THE EYE OF THE STORM

PART 3—THE TRIBE OF THE FOREST

UNDER THREAT

1

A Worrisome Disappearance

Vasco placed his front paws on the edge of the crate and stuck his head out. His snout raised, he happily breathed in the smells of the harbor—salt, fuel, burnt rubber, and rust—all of which indicated the presence of freighters. *There is no better place in the world than this for a young rat,* he thought as he stretched out his body. Each day humans dumped enough trash on the wharf to feed the entire tribe. Since his birth, Vasco had never known hunger. Life was easy for him. Eating and sleeping were all that he required.

Yet as the sun rose on the horizon, glimmers of dawn began to redden the harbor waters. The bustle of men would soon make this place too dangerous to linger around. It was time to go back.

His belly heavy with food, Vasco clumsily clambered up and passed through the hole in the crate. He fell onto the other side and scurried between the steel cables coiled on the wharf. Although he had never left the docks of the harbor, he felt more daring each day. This past night he had gone a little farther than usual from the nest. And who knew? Soon he might find the courage to go beyond the last landing dock, straight toward the city.

For the time being, though, he hurried along, impatient to rejoin his tribe and the safety of his nest. His mother, brothers, and all the others were waiting for him. He cleared a gangway, slipped through the moorings of a tugboat, and zigzagged between the huge legs of cranes. He could see the warehouse now and covered the last stretch at full speed. He coasted along a wall and turned at the corner before finding the twisted sheet of metal that his kind used as a door.

When he reached the opening, Vasco stopped, on the alert. A strange silence hung about the warehouse. Vasco sniffed the air with worry, on the lookout for danger. Picking up no particular signals, he ventured inside.

In the warehouse, everything was quiet . . . too quiet.

Vasco cautiously approached the opening in the pipe that led to the burrow. He sniffed an unfamiliar smell. It was not that of a cat, or of another rat, or of a human. It was a new smell, not altogether unpleasant.

Vasco hesitated and stood on his hind legs. Finally he slipped into the pipe and reached the corridor that had been dug under the warehouse. The unfamiliar smell was still there. But Vasco didn't detect the morning commotion that usually prevailed when he returned from hunting. Why weren't the females scurrying in all directions to feed their little ones?

Vasco grew increasingly concerned. Going deeper into the burrow, his snout forward, he explored each nook and cranny. He recognized the foul smells of urine, of droppings, and of food remnants. But where were the rats of his tribe? Vasco emitted a short cry and pricked up his ears. An icy silence made him shudder. His heart began beating madly. He let out another squeak, running this way, then that way, until he reached the end of the burrow. Now he had to acknowledge what he saw: there was no one around.

Vasco was seized with fear. He ran in circles, unable to make a decision. He thought of his mother and brothers and wished they would appear so he could take refuge among them. But nothing happened. The mysterious and frightening silence continued.

Panic-stricken, Vasco rushed toward the exit, knocking against the elbows of the pipe and hurting his flanks on the metal mesh installed by men to keep rats from going through. When he finally reached the ground floor of the warehouse, he ran outside to search for a sign, any trace, of his family.

Men were busy at work on the ships, but Vasco sprinted toward the end of the wharf. All of a sudden he noticed a small ball of gray fur lying between the wheels of an idle loading machine. His heart thumping, Vasco slipped under the vehicle. The ball of fur did not move. Vasco came nearer, sniffing at it. It was Memona, the oldest rat of his tribe. Full of hope, Vasco licked her snout and nudged her. She moved slightly. She wasn't dead! Vasco tried to calm his pounding heart by huddling close to her.

Memona was very weak. A strange dull smell emanated from her body. Vasco rubbed himself against her, trying to warm her up. She groaned and raised her head. At the sight of Vasco, a little bit of relief came to her half-closed and sad eyes.

"Where are the others?" Vasco asked.

Memona turned her head toward the warehouse. She no longer had the strength to speak.

"The nest is empty!" Vasco tried again. "Where are the others?"

Memona's head fell down, as heavy as a piece of wood. Vasco rubbed his snout on her panting flanks. She was breathing with difficulty. After a while, she opened her eyes again and raised her head. By the way she looked at Vasco, he understood that something awful had happened.

"Men . . . ," gasped the old rat.

Vasco leaped to his paws. Men had come! They had caught his tribe! But how? And why? He ran in circles around Memona, uttering squeaks of despair. But Memona seemed to ignore his cries. She was already somewhere else.

Gathering all her strength, Memona dragged herself across the paving stones, gripping the uneven surface of the ground to inch forward. She puffed. She groaned. Distraught, Vasco followed her. He didn't understand what was going on. Seeing Memona in pain made him feel helpless. He could only watch as the old rat crawled past the wheels of the machine and, in full view, made her way toward the edge of the wharf.

A few steps from the water, Memona's body stiffened. She could no longer move. Vasco brought his snout closer and gently nibbled her. Memona jerked slightly and extended her neck toward the water. An opaque veil came over her eyes, as if she were looking at the world through a thick glass window. She opened her mouth suddenly, showing the two worn canines of her lower jaw.

"They are all dead," she said. "And so am I. You're the last one."

Vasco shivered. He felt as if the ground had opened under his feet. "No," he murmured. "You can't leave me!"

Memona gave him a vacant look. "Be cautious of men. Of the steam . . . ," she warned.

Then the old rat sighed deeply and let her head fall down on the paving stones.

2

The Stranger

Vasco scratched Memona's flanks, hoping she would react. When nothing happened, he remembered seeing the corpse of a young female whose body had been crushed by a falling crate in the warehouse. He had sniffed her at length. A dull smell had wafted from her— the same dull smell that was coming from Memona's body. Vasco let out a piercing squeak from deep within his gut. He understood now that Memona would never move again.

At that moment, the howling of a foghorn gave him a

start. Through the wheels of a truck, Vasco could see the belly of a freighter glide by, slicing through the oil-slick waters of the harbor. It was daylight now. The sun had warmed up the ground.

Memona's last words rang in his head but he didn't understand their meaning. What steam was she talking about? How had men destroyed his entire tribe? The only thing Vasco knew for certain was that he was alone in the world. And that he could no longer stay here.

He grabbed one of Memona's ears between his teeth and began to drag her body. Where to go? He did not know. He felt angry and desperate.

The corpse was heavy and Vasco stumbled against the uneven paving stones. Pulling backward, he reached the edge of the wharf, his body arched from the effort. His paws scratched the ground and skidded, but he managed to lift the old rat onto the edge, just over the water. A few centimeters below, he discovered a hole large enough to accommodate two rats. He was about to pull Memona's body inside when the shouts of a man attracted his attention. They were followed by the squeaks of a frightened rat. Right behind the wheels of the truck, he could see the legs of a human. And between the legs, a rat was cornered against metal containers. The man, armed with a shovel, struck once, barely missing the rat.

Vasco instinctively sprang forward. He dashed under

the truck, and as the man was about to strike a second blow, Vasco bit down on his ankle.

The man howled in pain and surprise. He hardly had time to turn around before Vasco dug his teeth into the man's flesh through his pants. The man shook his leg, sending Vasco rolling. The other rat escaped and started running toward the edge of the wharf, while the man rushed toward Vasco in rage. The shovel came down in front of his snout. Vasco could smell the hot metal and the stench of human sweat. His heart beat madly. He jumped and scurried through the legs of his enemy, running toward the water. There he found the hole and rushed inside.

In the darkness, Vasco sensed the presence of the rat he had just saved. Vasco made himself small at the bottom of the hole, crowding against this stranger who still shook with terror. From the smell, Vasco realized that she was a young female. She made a move to flee but froze upon hearing the footsteps of the man above. The man grumbled and hit the paving stones with his shovel. Frightened, the rat hid near Vasco. Neither of them dared to breathe.

A moment of silence was followed by a scraping sound on the wharf.

The man shouted something.

Then Memona's lifeless body fell in front of the hole.

Vasco heard a splash. He rushed to the opening . . . just in time to see the corpse of the old rat disappear in the dark water.

The man spat with disgust before going away.

Vasco remained still, feeling dizzy. He was fascinated by the ripples the fall of Memona's body had created. The young rat finally joined him. In turn, she leaned over the water, shyly touching Vasco with the tips of her whiskers. He looked at her, startled. He had just saved her life and yet she was only a stranger! The rat seemed grateful but her eyes were full of questions. She did not understand why Vasco had come to her aid. The squeaks she was emitting were to warn other rats of the danger and make them flee.

Calm surrounded them once more. For a while, the two rats observed each other silently and sniffed each other's scent.

"My name is Nil," the female said finally.

Vasco already knew that she did not live among the tribes of the harbor. Her olfactory signs were unknown to him. She more likely came from the city and had probably gotten separated from her group during the nighttime hunting.

Nil pointed her snout outside and sniffed in the direction of the wind, clearly eager to leave this hostile spot and find her place again among her own tribe. Before leaving, she turned to Vasco as if inviting him to follow her.

With Nil gone, Vasco looked down at the harbor water. He was unable to think properly. A shiver went through his spine. What was the good of staying on the harbor? He had no ties to anyone anymore. His whole life had changed now that his family was dead. All of a sudden, he decided that he would follow Nil.

Scampering onto the wharf, Vasco spotted Nil as she headed into a storm drain behind the warehouse. He quickly caught up with her and rushed into the dark labyrinth of the town sewer.

3

Into the Belly of the City

Vasco and Nil moved rapidly through the sewer system. The daylight grew weaker the farther down they went, and the coat of limestone that covered the walls thickened. In some places the sewers resembled grottos. Greenish stalactites hung from the roof of the tunnels. Vasco could see the tail of his companion swinging rhythmically in front of him. He breathed in the smell of stagnant water, mud, and rusted metal. Soon his eyes would be of no help. He would have to rely on his sense of smell and the tactile ability of his whiskers.

Yet Nil kept going south at a quick speed, and Vasco

followed along the narrow pipes like a sleepwalker. Some pipes were damaged, and from time to time water gushed through the holes. After a few hundred meters, both rats were drenched.

Suddenly Nil stopped. She stood on her hind legs, her snout in the air. Several drainage pipes converged on that spot and poured into a larger drain. Cornices bordered the flood tide of the frothy, nauseatingly dirty water. Farther away, Vasco could hear the swirl of the pumping station.

Looking to make sure the way was safe, Nil moved ahead, balancing on the cornice. She glanced back to encourage Vasco to do the same.

Vasco sprang forward and the two rats continued to head south. Vasco couldn't stop thinking about the morning's events. He wanted to go back to the peaceful moment when he had been contemplating the harbor, when the members of his tribe were still alive and everything had still been possible.

When they reached a fork in the tunnel, Nil climbed over a large concrete pipe that angled slightly upward. Vasco ascended the pipe in turn and felt a kind of diffuse heat under his paws.

Here the smells were so fetid they made him choke. An intricate network of metal ducts and electrical wires branched out toward the surface. Men were not far away. Nil sniffed the walls with care. She seemed relieved to

13

find the familiar site impregnated with the scent of her people. Nil's tribe had established their quarters under an apartment building, right behind the room of garbage cans, where food was plentiful.

The closer he got to the foundations of the building, the more Vasco slowed down. He was increasingly uncomfortable at the idea of encountering unknown rats. After all, he was far from the harbor now, far from everything he knew. This place didn't smell of salt or fish. It smelled of humans, gasoline, and rotting meat. What was he going to do in a tribe so different from his own?

A few centimeters away, Nil slipped behind a copper sheet. Vasco froze. He sensed danger. Nil walked back impatiently. She touched Vasco lightly with the ends of her whiskers.

"Come on," she insisted.

She pushed him toward the copper sheet but Vasco resisted. In the dark, both rats caught their breath. Vasco could hear his blood beat in his temples. Nil was still very young. She didn't know the cruelty with which rats sometimes treated their fellow creatures. As for him, he had already witnessed deadly fights between tribes in the harbor. He knew that one didn't enter a new nest without paying a price.

"I can't go in," he said finally. "I'm a stranger."

"But you saved my life," Nil answered. "Besides, you're all alone. Why don't you hide while I explain to them what—"

Suddenly Nil's ears pricked up. She remained motionless, listening for noises and sniffing for smells. Vasco also sensed a change in the air. It was coming from the hot-water pipe. He heard grating noises on the concrete. Then a strong odor of rotten meat and blood reached his nostrils. A draft from the sewer brought the signal of danger. Nil picked it up too. She started trembling and running nervously around Vasco.

"We can't stay here!" she shouted. "Come, there is another way in!"

She slipped under the copper sheet. Vasco rushed behind her without hesitation.

Both rats entered into a hole dug through the ground and soon reached a larger hole. At the other end was the entrance to Nil's nest. Above them, a corridor went up.

"This way!" Nil said. "Quick!"

Vasco brushed against Nil's flanks and impregnated himself with her scent. Then he turned and entered the corridor. He had made a decision: he was not going to stay here.

The younger rat let out two separate high-pitched squeaks of a particular frequency.

Vasco stopped running and answered her with two identical cries. Perhaps one day this signal would allow them to meet again. But for now Vasco had to hurry. He fled through the ground corridor.

● ● ●

Right then, a horde of noisy and smelly rats tumbled down the hole. The leader was a huge male with a dark brown coat. He limped toward the entrance to the nest. It was Akar, the dominant rat of Nil's tribe. Each night he went out accompanied by his hunters. They would raid the sewers, gnawing at everything in their path. Wood partitions, brick walls—nothing stopped them. When they entered basements, they devoured food stocks and ripped open garbage bags. It was all done in fun, and also to frighten the rats of other tribes who dared venture into their territory.

When he passed by Nil, Akar gave her a scornful look. He did not like weaklings. Nil had failed during the hunt; she had gotten lost. It had been her first hunt, but still . . . She looked down submissively.

Akar grunted. The other males filed behind him, dragging their bounty of food to the nest. Nil stayed to observe them. She knew that none of these rats would have had the courage to attack the man in the harbor. None of them would have had Vasco's intensely sad look upon seeing Memona's body fall into the dark water.

Vasco was right to flee, she told herself.

4

The Survivors

Vasco climbed the steep corridor. His claws dug into the ground like clamps. He was out of breath but felt relieved that he had left. Soon he saw a light at the end of the tunnel. He hurried and managed to reach a concrete slab. Above him, a grate let in more light. It had not rained for a few days and the catch basin was dry. Vasco crouched down, then sprang toward the opening.

He was frightened when he put his head outside. Dozens of humans were walking in all directions. Cars grazed the curbs and rolled past the grate, leaving behind a smell of gasoline and overheated tires. It was life on the street.

Vasco retreated behind the grate to observe the scene. The street was totally different from the harbor. The pace was much faster. Humans were so plentiful they seemed to control their territory like soldiers. Yet Vasco couldn't turn back. He took advantage of a slowdown in traffic and jumped out.

Once on the sidewalk, he ran. Feet, legs, baby carriage wheels, feet, legs . . . A swirl of new odors, noises, and colors assailed Vasco's senses. But he kept running blindly, straight ahead. Some humans shouted and jumped aside when they saw him, others tried to chase him and crush him with their heel. Vasco thought he was done for when a man cornered him against a wall and sprayed something on his snout. His skin started to itch and his eyes began to burn. With effort, he managed to escape. He ran, jumped, hugged the walls, crossed a street, and turned into another, his heart tight with fear. At last, he noticed an air vent and slithered into it, breathless.

The air vent opened onto a basement. Vasco curled up on top of a shelf. Fortunately, the effects of the spray were dwindling and the irritation was less painful. Soon he regained his spirits. Odors of grain, saltpeter, and fermentation tickled his nostrils. He felt a knot in his stomach. He was hungry.

As Vasco was about to crawl down from the shelf, he spotted another rat. This meant he would have to fight for any food, but he felt ready. His muscles tensed, his breath slowed down, and acrid saliva filled his mouth. He got ready to pounce on his adversary, but then another rat entered the basement—and then another, and another, and another. Soon a whole colony of black rats emerged from a hole in the wall. Faced with so many rats, Vasco abandoned any thought of fighting. He didn't dare move. He just curled up again on the shelf and watched as, one after the other, the black rats began gnawing at the canvas of a flour bag. The inexperienced younger rats buried their snouts in the powder and emerged all white, squealing with frustration. Meanwhile the adults sat on their haunches and caught the flour with their front paws.

To watch such a feast unravel under his nose and not be able to participate was torture for Vasco. He turned and looked at the street through the air vent. The harbor was not that far away. Even on his own, he would probably find shelter and food.

So Vasco left the basement and resumed his mad run along the city streets. Danger and hunger made him fly. He avoided the cars and hid behind the garbage cans on the sidewalks. He didn't even stop to explore them, fearing that a human would take advantage of it to catch him. His sense of smell told him in what direction the harbor lay.

When he approached the wharf, he crossed an empty lot, then went over some railroad tracks. At last, he found some trash to nibble on: greasy papers, cigarette butts, vegetable peels that smelled of meat. His hunger less acute, he ran toward an asphalted area. The smell of the sea attracted him like a magnet. Even from this distance he could discern the heavy shapes of cranes and freighters. He was no longer afraid.

At the harbor, he hid behind a pile of crates and watched his warehouse. Its metal roof, whitened by the salt air, sparkled in the sun, and suddenly he longed to revisit the premises. He scurried to the opening and slid behind the sheet of twisted metal.

Inside, he again sniffed the strange and pleasant smell that permeated what had been his nest. But he was wary and ignored the pipe, choosing to pass over a tarp that was behind a pile of planks. He took a complete tour of the warehouse and found nothing. His tribe had left no trace. It was as if they had vanished.

Suddenly Vasco heard squeals—the sharp, strong squeals of young rats. They were coming from under the tarp.

Vasco slid under it. Among tools and the spare parts of an engine, he discovered three small rats clinging to one another. He sniffed at them. They were young rats from his tribe.

"What are you doing here?" he asked, stupefied.

He remembered their names—the two males were called Hog and Coben, and the female was named Tiel. They had come from the same litter. They were still young, but capable of moving without their mother. It was probably what had saved their lives.

The young rats recognized Vasco's scent and rubbed themselves against him.

"We're hungry," moaned the little female.

"Bring us back to the nest," Hog begged.

Vasco swayed his head from right to left. Should he abandon them to their fate, as any other rat would do? No, he didn't have the stomach to do that. They were so young. Vasco knew that these rats would not survive on their own. The most urgent thing was to leave this place before men came to collect their equipment.

Pushing them with the tip of his snout, Vasco showed the young rats the exit and directed them toward the twisted metal sheet. Where was he taking them? The sewers? The streets?

The three young rats jostled one another outside. They found a piece of string and tore and gnawed at it, uttering high-pitched squeals of pleasure. At this hour, the sun cast a reddish color on the ships in the harbor. Everything seemed so tranquil. . . . But Vasco knew that many dangers appeared without warning. If he didn't find shelter for the young rats, they might die.

He mulled over all the distressing things that had

happened to him since the morning. He too would be relieved if he could sleep in a nest. But only females knew how to build one. Vasco concluded that there was only one solution. *It's risky, but what else can I do?* he thought.

He gathered the young rats and pushed them toward the storm drain behind the warehouse.

"Come on!" he said. "Follow me!"

And so Vasco left the harbor, knowing that his former life had ended.

5

The King of Resourcefulness

Vasco tried to remember which way Nil had taken him. Had she gone south or west? His recollection was fuzzy. Unsure, he dragged the three rats along in the dark. They followed narrow pipes for a while, then Vasco got the feeling that he recognized the route.

Behind him, the young ones had resumed their games. This was an adventure for them, and they thought only of having fun. Tiel and Hog were pushing and shoving each other at the risk of falling down. Vasco gave them a little warning with his paw. The two rats looked confused and quieted down.

At last they reached the sewer.

Yes, that's the sewer, all right, Vasco thought. *It seems larger, more turbulent, but it's very likely the right one.*

When they got to the end of the concrete drain, Vasco showed the young ones how to jump on the cornice that ran along the water. Tiel and Coben managed successfully. But Hog got a bad start; his paws slipped, and he fell in the water. Vasco sent out a shrill cry and scrutinized the surface. Quickly Hog reappeared.

"Swim!" Vasco shouted to him. "We'll fish you out farther down!"

Like all rats, Hog was an excellent swimmer. He kept his snout above the water as the strong current carried him along faster and faster. Vasco and the two others were running quickly along the edge but were losing ground. At one of the turns in the canal, Hog suddenly disappeared.

Vasco turned to look at Tiel and Coben. "Jump!" he ordered them.

Without hesitation, he dove into the canal and let himself flow with the current. The two young rats dove in after him.

The water was dark, cold, and sticky. Trash floated on the surface, swirling around. Past the turn, the canal went down a stone tunnel that smelled of moss and urine. Vasco swam with his front legs to gain speed. But it was too dark to catch sight of Hog.

Vasco's head suddenly knocked against an obstacle. He squeaked in pain. Tiel and Coben hurt themselves against this rigid surface too. It was a metal grid that barred the way. Hog was trapped there as well. He gripped Vasco's fur as the current pushed them against the crossbars. The grid also stopped a lot of trash from flowing: tin cans, plastic bottles, pieces of cardboard, branches, paper, and spongy stuff that could no longer be identified.

"We have to go underneath!" Vasco shouted.

He dove into the water and went down along the grid, but it was sealed at the bottom—impossible to go through. Using his sharp teeth, Vasco tried to gnaw at the metal crossbars, but he quickly got discouraged and came back up to the surface to breathe. The trash carried by the canal arrived like missiles. Leaving this place was a must.

Vasco signaled to the others that they had to turn back. They started to swim against the current, amid the deafening noise of the swirling water, but the rats were too young and lacked the strength. They were soon exhausted and found themselves crushed against the grid again. Panic was about to overtake Vasco when he heard a groan above him—a groan followed by the squeal of a rat. He looked up.

A rat was watching them. Vasco could see him thanks to a glimmer of light coming from an air vent. The rat was perched high in a dry duct, from which he surveyed the scene.

"Looks like you're in trouble," the rat said, sounding amused.

Vasco was startled. The stranger indicated the trash that was piling higher and higher against the grid. Of course! It was from the top that they could extricate themselves from this maelstrom.

Vasco swam toward Hog and used his snout to push him until the young rat grabbed hold of a dead branch. Then Vasco pushed him a little higher. Hog's paws found the holes in the grid, and he used the metal crossbars like the rungs of a ladder.

"You're doing good, little one!" the stranger commented. "Come this way."

As Hog climbed up, Vasco pulled Tiel and Coben from the water. Balanced on top of the trash pile, he looked at them as they climbed the grid. When the three young ones were safely in the dry duct, Vasco quickly joined them. Dripping, he faced the strange rat, who looked at him mischievously. He seemed a little older than Vasco, and his beige fur hid strong muscles.

"Thank you," Vasco said, catching his breath. He turned toward the young ones. "We have to keep going."

The beige rat whistled lightly. "You seem in a hurry," he said. "But these little ones are exhausted."

"And famished!" Tiel chimed in tiredly.

The beige rat pointed his snout outside. His eyes were

shining. "What would you say to taking part in a delicious feast?"

The three rats looked at Vasco, who hesitated. Vasco did not appreciate the arrogant manners of this stranger, but a strong smell of garbage and carrion emanated from him, a mixture that seemed to confirm that he knew places where food was abundant.

The beige rat raised his head toward the surface again and gave a few sniffs. His whiskers quivered.

"My name is Regus," he said. "Regus, the king of resourcefulness!"

Without warning, Regus turned his back on Vasco and entered a tunnel going up. The three young ones followed him, listening only to their stomachs. Vasco sighed in resignation. The beige rat seemed harmless. And, to be honest, Vasco needed to regain his strength as well.

6

In Rats' Paradise

Regus came out of the sewer first. He made sure there was no danger and then signaled for the others to follow him. Vasco and the young rats emerged into a back alley. Darkness had come a long time ago, but the place was lit by the neighboring streetlights. Dozens of rats ran around, bustling around the trash. A huge waste bin stood against the back wall. *This is an excellent address!* Vasco told himself as he breathed in the smell of rotting meat that floated temptingly in the air.

"All the restaurants in the area throw their trash in

this bin," Regus explained. "We're safe as long as cats or dogs don't show up."

But Vasco was suspicious. The other rats might attack them to defend their territory. He held Tiel back as the young rat was about to enter the fray.

Yet Regus crossed the yard. He seemed at home. He climbed over a pile of old boxes, then clung to one of the downspouts, and finally jumped into the bin. The other rats didn't make a move, so Vasco and the little ones advanced timidly.

"Don't be afraid!" Regus encouraged them when he reappeared at the top of the bin. "You're my guests! The others will leave you alone!"

Vasco and the young ones climbed over the boxes and jumped into the bin. It was only half full but what was there was particularly appetizing: bits of pizza, shreds of chicken meat attached to the bones, almost-fresh fish heads, stale bread, and all kinds of greasy papers, which in themselves would make a decent meal. Rats milled around in the middle of the trash. Some were skinny and bald, others were as fat as lab animals. But none of them was aggressive.

While the young attacked a pork bone, Vasco joined Regus. For a while, they devoured all they could find. There was no better way for rats to get acquainted than to share a feast.

"Where are you going with the three little ones?" Regus asked finally.

"We had a tribe in the harbor," Vasco explained. "The others have disappeared. I have to find shelter for the young ones."

His whiskers glistening with grease, Regus looked at Vasco with interest. Vasco then told him about Memona's death, her mysterious message, and the strange smell in the warehouse.

"A strange smell . . . ," Regus repeated. "Hmmm."

He resumed tearing his meat while Vasco continued.

"I'm taking them to a new tribe. I was trying to find my way but got lost."

Again Regus seemed amused. "A tribe!" He laughed. "What for?"

Vasco looked at his companion in surprise. He had never met such a strange rat. His elders had always told him that the only way to survive was to integrate into a community and follow its rules. A tribeless rat was certain to die. And yet here, right in front of him, was a rat who didn't look at things the same way.

"Do you live on your own?" Vasco dared to ask.

Regus sat on his hind legs and began licking his paws. "Living in a tribe is for imbeciles," he declared.

Then he told Vasco about his life as a solitary rat, about the freedom and the exhilaration to go wherever he wanted, without having to worry about anything but his own happiness and comfort. Vasco had to admit that Regus did not look famished or in bad health. Living alone and without ties, Regus was knowledgeable about the whole town, the sewers as well as the surface, the street hazards, and the traps set by man.

"Men use their intelligence to fight us," Regus declared. "Thwarting their inventions amuses me."

Perplexed, Vasco dug in a box and retrieved a chunk of pizza crust seething with maggots. He sank his teeth into it, all the while looking at Regus from the corner of his eyes. For sure, this was no ordinary rat. And he just might be right.

But then squeaks distracted Vasco from his thoughts. Hog had stolen a piece of fish from Tiel and a fight started. Tiel threw herself on Hog's back. She scratched him, biting him violently. Hog struggled and sent his sister rolling down to the bottom of the waste bin, between some clumps of paper. Vasco looked at Regus.

"I can't live without a tribe," he said. "I have the little ones now. They need protection."

"As you wish." Regus sighed. "In which tribe would you like to seek refuge? I can take you there. I know them all."

"I met a young female rat on the harbor. Her name is Nil."

When he heard the name, Regus became gloomy. "Nil? Of Akar's tribe?"

Vasco nodded. Regus seemed troubled but made no comment. He lifted his snout outside the bin. Dawn was approaching.

"Akar and his hunters will soon be returning from their nocturnal expedition. If you really want to try your luck with them, you've got to go now."

Vasco gathered the three young rats, who were worn out from having eaten so much. It took a lot of energy to persuade them to leave the smelly paradise of the bin.

At last, the three youngsters jumped down into the alley. On the way, Vasco grabbed a fish head. He planned to offer it to Nil; that was the least he could do.

Regus led the file. Underground, from pipes to ducts, he took Vasco up to the copper sheet marking the boundary of Akar's territory.

"I won't go any farther," he declared. "But should you need me, you can always find me around."

Vasco was about to push the young ones behind the sheet when Regus called him back.

"Don't mention me to anyone. Not even to Nil. You don't know me."

Without trying to understand why, Vasco swore to keep the secret. Then, he slid toward the hole, dragging the fish. The young ones scurried in front of him.

"Be careful of Akar," Regus added.

He turned to go back the way he had come—back to his solitary life in the nameless obscurity of the sewers.

7

An Audacious Request

His senses on the alert, Vasco cautiously allowed the three young rats to approach the hole. He felt reassured that he knew the escape route in case of an emergency. But everything seemed quiet. As Regus had anticipated, Akar probably hadn't returned from his hunt yet.

Vasco approached the entrance to Nil's nest. He inhaled its scent. Then he gave two high-pitched squeaks, hoping that Nil would recognize their signal.

A few seconds later, he heard a noise in the hole. Small rat steps loosened grains of soil and sand. Soon Nil appeared. She nosed up to Vasco with the tips of her whiskers.

"Glad to see you again," she greeted him.

Vasco was reassured by her welcome and walked back to the bottom of the hole, where the young ones were waiting. He pushed them toward Nil with his snout. Hog, Tiel, and Coben stood close together.

"I need help," Vasco said. "These little ones have no one else but me to protect them."

Nil trotted around the little rats suspiciously. She touched them with her whiskers, poked at them with her snout, and finally looked at Vasco.

"Four rats are a far cry from one!" she said.

"I know," Vasco agreed. "It's because of them that I need you."

He drew closer to Nil and tried to coax her. But he sensed her nervousness and indecision. She circled the rats and explained her reaction.

"I spoke to Akar," she said. "He refuses to take you in."

Coben huddled near Vasco. "Then we have nowhere to sleep?" said the young rat.

Nil stopped. She exhaled a scent of fear. Vasco did not speak; he did not want to pressure her.

"There may still be a way to have you accepted," Nil murmured. "Don't move!"

She went back to her nest, leaving Vasco without any explanation.

• • •

While Vasco and the three young ones waited in the hole, Nil hurried along a lengthy horizontal tunnel. Then she crossed a communal room that was deserted at this time of the night. From there, she turned left to another corridor and passed several nests before finally arriving in the largest room of the burrow. The whole tribe was assembled as they waited for the return of the hunters. But already Nil smelled the odor of meat.

It was a dead pigeon. In the center of the room, a huge female was rubbing her paws in front of the feathered corpse. It was Ourga, the dominant female, who with Akar headed up the tribe. Around her were a few rats, the strongest of the tribe. Suddenly Ourga bared her teeth—two sharp incisors that stuck out of her jaw like butchers' knives.

The whole tribe held its breath as Ourga dug her teeth into the pigeon flesh. Immediately the bigger rats entered the fray. There were squeaks and squeals, scratching and biting. Each one wanted his or her share, and to get it a rat had to be ready to do anything.

Nil could join the pack and participate in this royal feast, but she wasn't being led by hunger. She was looking for a couple of rats who could help Vasco. She saw them at last: Lek, the male, stood on his hind legs and watched from a distance the meal of his fellow rats. Behind him was Joun, his female. She too stayed away, with her four little ones by her side.

Nil approached them shyly. She was not very familiar with them because Nil belonged to the dominant group of rats close to Akar. Lek and Joun did not. Only when Ourga satisfied her appetite would the other rats be allowed to come near the pigeon and feed their little ones. That was the law.

Nil faced Lek and spoke with effort. "Lek . . . I have something to show you."

Looking surprised, Lek dropped down onto four legs. "To me?" he asked.

Nil nodded. "You have to come to the entrance of the burrow."

Lek glanced at Joun, who was having a hard time keeping her famished brood in check. They squeaked and stamped their paws, tempted by the smell of the meat. In the middle of the room, the dominant rats were still noisily fighting over the pieces of flesh, amid the sound of breaking bones and shrieks. Pigeon feathers flew around them.

"This morning a rat from another tribe saved my life, and—" Nil began.

"I know," Lek said.

"This rat is at the entrance of our burrow."

Lek looked at Nil with a puzzled expression. Since morning, the story of Nil's rescue on the harbor had traveled around the burrow. A rat capable of such courage was no ordinary rat. Lek told Nil that he would like to see him, but he was afraid of Akar's reaction if the leader came upon them. However, Nil insisted, so after a moment of hesitation Lek followed her.

• • •

With fear in his belly, Lek followed Nil away from the group. He was always gripped by this fear in his gut—as if it were a painful and living organ. It was this fear that dictated his behavior, made him tremble, and kept him from abandoning the tribe forever. Several times Joun had begged him to leave. There would be enough food somewhere else for their family. But Lek didn't have the courage to make a change. He yielded to Akar's will, to his power, and to the small pittance that the tyrant allocated to him.

And yet Nil had sought him out.

So he crept across the burrow, silent as a shadow, in spite of his fear.

8

Facing Akar

On the threshold of the burrow, Vasco grew impatient. Time and again he went to sniff at the scents that rose from the sewers, making sure that no danger lurked.

"It's not for you!" Vasco snapped as the three young rats, squeaking with hunger, flipped the fish over. "Don't touch it."

The fish was not for them. The nest was not for them either. Would these rats find a shelter or were they condemned to die? Vasco didn't have answers and grew angry.

Fortunately, Nil returned at last. An adult rat, rather skinny, followed her and looked at Vasco and the little ones in surprise.

"This is Lek," Nil announced. "You can trust him."

But when Vasco explained the situation to him, Lek's expression grew scared.

"We can't take you in," he said. "We already don't have enough food for our own little ones. Four more mouths—it's impossible!"

"But I can hunt!" Vasco protested. "I'll bring back my share of food."

To give weight to his words, Vasco fetched the fish and placed it under Lek's nose.

Lek sniffed at the fish and cast a sad glance at Vasco as he tried to explain that Akar confiscated all the food for himself and those of his inner circle. Looking depressed and ashamed, Lek turned, as if to go back to the burrow, but Nil held him in place.

"Are you that afraid of Akar?" she asked.

"If *you're* not afraid of him, then why did you come to me?" Lek replied. "I have no power here and you know it!"

Nil lowered her head and did not answer. At the bottom of the hole, the three young ones huddled together and went to sleep. Vasco looked at them. An irrepressible force told him he had to protect them.

"I want to meet your chief," he murmured. "I'll find a way to convince him. I'll put myself at his service if necessary."

Suddenly, Lek gave a start and Nil jumped up. They had just detected a very familiar scent. Within moments a noisy procession of paws and panting breaths could be heard in the corridor leading to the burrow.

"Akar," Nil whispered.

As Lek retreated toward the darkest corner, where the young rats had taken refuge, Vasco stayed resolutely by Nil's trembling side. He got a whiff of the warm and damp smell that preceded the hunters.

All of a sudden, a group of rats with dripping fur surged into the hole. There were about half a dozen, all of them carrying morsels of bread, discarded meat, worms, and even pieces of soap in their mouths. They brought the scent of smoke, tar, and gasoline with them. Akar marched at the back of his victorious army. He had rough fur and shiny eyes, and there was blood on his snout and whiskers. He was huge, but he limped. He was barely in the hole when he stood on his hind legs, made a noise of disgust, and then let out a hoarse cry.

Vasco tried to calm his furiously beating heart and took two steps toward Akar before flattening himself on the ground in a sign of submission. The hunters surrounded him.

Akar came near and sniffed noisily at the intruder.

"This stranger stinks," he shouted.

A sour taste came to Vasco's throat. He didn't move.

"This is Vasco," Nil said courageously. "The rat I told you about this morning. The one who saved my life in the harbor."

Akar turned to her, silencing her in one commanding look. The circle of hunters closed in. His snout to the ground, Vasco could hardly contain his fright. He could feel the fur rise on his back.

"I have come to offer my services," he said. "If you allow me to join your tribe, I'll be an excellent hunter."

A heavy silence followed as Akar kept his eyes on Vasco's arched back. Then Lek entered the circle, dragging the fish toward the chief.

"Vasco brought you this," he said, his voice shaky. "It is proof that he—"

Lek did not have time to finish his sentence. Claws out, Akar gave him a blow to the head, scratching him deeply. Lek moaned and went back to hide at the bottom of the hole. Yet Akar sniffed the fish and, without a word, started eating it. They could all hear the noise of the bones and cartilage breaking under the voracious teeth of the huge rat. This went on for a while. Then Akar licked his whiskers.

"I already have hunters," he pronounced. "Strangers are not welcome in my tribe!"

Vasco sensed that he was losing ground. If he couldn't

convince Akar of his worthiness, he'd have to fight. And under these conditions it would be a lost battle.

"I know places where food is plentiful," he insisted. "Far from here . . ."

Akar swished his tail, making an irritating friction noise. His hunters were only waiting for their chief's command to pounce and evict the stranger from their territory. But Akar evidently realized the advantages that he could derive from Vasco's proposal.

"Ourga, my female, is always hungry. Always very hungry!" he said in a heavy voice. "Bring another fish and maybe I'll take you into the tribe. For a while . . ."

Vasco raised his head in front of the massive and frightening Akar. He breathed faster.

"I'll bring back what you ask for. Before dawn, your female will have her fish."

Without further comment, Akar passed in front of him and went deep into his burrow. The hunters disappeared behind him, carrying the loot of the night.

• • •

In the hole, Nil sighed with relief. Lek observed Vasco with admiration; he had the feeling that by joining the tribe, this rat might shatter all its rules. This feeling scared him at the same time that it exhilarated him. It was a feeling that he had long ago forgotten. Not since the death of Lod, the former chief of the tribe, had he felt this way.

"Take care of the young ones," Vasco told Lek and Nil. "I'll be back!" He bolted through the corridor.

"Joun will take good care of them!" Lek shouted after him. "Don't worry!"

9

The Solitary Hunt

Vasco ascended the corridor at full speed, passed over the concrete slab, and jumped outside through the grate. At this time of night, traffic was light and passers-by were practically absent from the sidewalks. For one who had been exposed to the dangers of daylight, this nocturnal hunt looked like a stroll.

Vasco started to run, his snout in the air, looking for Regus' waste bin. He hugged the walls, going from street to street, ignoring the air vents at the bottom of apartment buildings. From time to time, the lights of a passing car swept the asphalt, tires screeched, men called out to each other—nothing really dangerous.

The pleasure of running went to Vasco's head. He gladly breathed in the cool night air, with the vague notion that this freedom would not last long. As he slipped through the chain-link fences surrounding empty lots, he thought of Regus. He too wanted to live alone, without restraint. It had to be pleasant.

Soon Vasco recognized the restaurant behind which the bin was located. The patrons had gone to bed a long time ago, the iron gates were down, everything was quiet. Taking no precautions, Vasco slipped under the porch and entered the enclosed alley. The bin was in full view—and full of promise. The rats who had been running in the area earlier had vanished. Vasco concentrated on his mission.

He climbed on top of the boxes and jumped into the bin. The trash exhaled a stench of rot and mildew within which Vasco tried to detect the smell of fish. With his front paws he pushed away cardboard and peels and dug deeper into the belly of the bin. At the bottom, he got an iodine whiff of fish. Sure enough, he found one that was almost whole. Surely this would please Akar's female.

Vasco grabbed the fish between his teeth and climbed to the top of the trash pile. He thought that if he fulfilled his mission, entry into the tribe wouldn't be very costly after all. Then he stopped. He discerned a presence in the dark. Had the rats come back? His muscles tense, Vasco listened, ready to take flight. Yet the alley remained silent. But Vasco was sure that someone was there. Slowly, without dropping the fish, he stood up to look over the edge of the bin. Several pairs of eyes shined back at him. They were not rats . . . they were cats.

Vasco felt the fur rise on his back and the knots of fear in his belly. Still, he couldn't wait. He planted his teeth firmly in the flesh of the fish and jumped out of the bin like a jack-in-the-box.

Caught by surprise, the cats let Vasco dash across the alley. But they quickly identified their prey and chased after him. In a few steps, they overtook him.

Vasco curled up, cornered against a wall. His enemies were circling him, slowly. They mewed, spat, and arched their backs. One of them suddenly reached out to give him a blow with his paw. Vasco jumped aside and avoided it, but another cat threw himself at him, his jaws wide open. The fear of dying electrified Vasco. He dropped the fish and rushed between the cat's legs, zigzagging, losing control of his breath and of his trajectory. He brushed past a wall, tried to climb up a downspout, and fell back down on the head of a cat, who mewed with rage. Again Vasco escaped. But it was so dark, he was completely disoriented. Finally he took off toward the waste bin, chased by three cats. As they were about to dig their claws into him, Vasco slipped under a pile of boxes. The cats rushed on top of the pile, making it collapse. One of the boxes turned over onto Vasco and pinned him down. Panic-stricken, he squeaked and began to squirm madly beneath his prison. The cats came back on the attack. Vasco could feel their warm breath. They hissed and pushed the box with their paws. As they lifted it, Vasco took off. He got scratched once on his back but managed to flee.

A light suddenly appeared in the alley. The tumult of the fight had woken up men. Windows opened, shouts were heard. Someone poured a bucket of water from the second floor. Drenched, the cats wailed in panic. Vasco took advantage of the confusion: he spotted a storm drain. He leaped to recover the fish that he had abandoned, grabbed it in his mouth, and dashed again through the alley. But the openings in the grate were too narrow for him to push the fish through. He felt a violent burning sensation on his back—the cats had caught up with him. In desperation, he pushed with all his strength, until the fish finally went inside.

Vasco fell into the dark duct as well. His head banged against the concrete panel, and he tumbled along the downward slope until a horizontal landing stopped his fall. He was saved.

He stayed still for a moment, not knowing whether he was dead or alive. His body shook and his back hurt. He could smell his own blood.

After a while, Vasco put the fish down and licked his wounds. He wanted nothing more than to rest and nibble on a morsel of his bounty, but he got up. He had to go back to Nil and Lek as soon as possible.

He crossed dark corridors, went over damp ducts where men's fetid trash had piled up, and realized with apprehension that this underground world was going to be his from now on.

He was exhausted when he approached the burrow. And when he went beyond the copper sheet that marked the entrance to the hole, his only wish was to sleep in the shelter of a nest.

Nil and Lek were still there, guarding the young ones. When Vasco appeared with the fish between his teeth, Nil rushed toward him.

"You succeeded!" she cried happily. But her mood grew somber when she discovered Vasco's wounds.

"It's nothing," he said weakly. "Take me to Ourga."

While Lek woke the young ones up, Vasco followed Nil through the long horizontal corridor. He was so tired that he was unable to think. Nil took him to the communal room, where the dominant rats were devouring their share of food. At the center, Ourga and Akar were sharing the best pieces of meat, making noises of pleasure.

Vasco went up to them and placed the fish on the ground.

Immediately the two dominant rats stopped eating and turned to him. Tempted, Ourga took a step closer, a little suspicious. Then without a gesture of appreciation she snatched up the fish and carried it away.

"Your offer is accepted," Akar stated. "You can stay with your young ones. But in exchange, you'll have to bring food back each night. A lot of food! If not, I'll chase you out."

"I thank you, Akar," Vasco whispered, swallowing his pride.

Without delay, Lek took Vasco and the young rats to his nest. Joun and her little ones were nibbling on a piece of soap. Vasco got closer to them and spat out a piece of fish that he had kept hidden in his cheek.

"This is for you," he said to Joun.

As he fell asleep, Vasco could hear the squeaks of all the little ones sharing his gift with glee.

10

A New Life

Life in the tribe was not easy for Vasco. Caring for the young ones required his complete attention during the day. Coben was well behaved, but Hog and Tiel could not stay still. Joun gave them as much food and attention as she gave her own young ones, but she couldn't meet all their demands. Her nest was too small for them.

As soon as Hog and Tiel ventured into the nooks of the burrow, the other rats chased them. Even Nil's repeated interventions didn't prevent them from getting their flanks scratched or bitten. So the two rats began to explore outside the burrow, in the human territory above. They discovered new ways of reaching the garbage room and didn't hesitate to climb the stairs to the landings.

Vasco watched over them diligently and taught them how to separate good seeds from the poisoned ones that men dispersed at the corners of walls. He showed them how traps functioned, taking care to explain how dangerous it was to come too close to humans. Unfortunately, Tiel and Hog were quick to forget his advice, and Vasco had to watch them constantly to ensure their safety.

• • •

Nighttime was for hunting.

Akar had forbidden Vasco from joining his group. He tolerated his presence in the burrow but couldn't abide his company during the nocturnal expeditions. So Vasco did his best to avoid him and went hunting alone, well beyond Akar's territory.

He learned to fight, to hide, and to recognize friends and enemies. Soon he navigated the sewers as easily as he did the surface, and even managed to prevail during confrontations. But extreme exhaustion was the price he paid. Every morning when he dropped his share of food at Akar's feet, he nearly fell asleep on the spot.

Yet Vasco never forgot to bring back a surprise for Lek

and Joun, whether a bird's egg, a piece of meat, or a crust of bread—a treat that he kept from Ourga's ravenous appetite.

Nil came to visit them every day. She too managed to divert a little bit of food. Akar kept an eye on her but she didn't care. It seemed to Vasco that in the short time he had known Nil, she had gone from being submissive and fearful to daring to anger Akar.

• • •

One evening, as Vasco was getting ready to hunt, Coben met him at the exit of the burrow.

"I want to come with you," said the young rat.

Surprised, Vasco stopped on the threshold. He refused.

"If we were two, you wouldn't be as tired," Coben insisted.

"If we were two, we would be twice as slow."

"Take me to the docks, to the harbor!"

"We have nothing to do with the harbor anymore," Vasco murmured. "Go back to Joun."

Vasco was about to leave when he noticed the sadness in the young rat's eyes. It was a misty, opaque gaze that reminded him of Memona on the day she died. Vasco sat on his hind legs, facing Coben. Musky smells filled his memory—smells of the harbor, of his tribe that had disappeared, of the nests of the females after they had given birth to blind and hairless newborns so little that the slightest blow would break their bones.

Vasco realized how alien he felt in this new place. *We need a tribe*, he thought. *A tribe that is ours*.

A concert of sharp cries, followed by the noise of heavy trodding, startled the two rats. There was no doubt about it: Akar and his hunters were returning.

Coben abandoned his pleas to accompany Vasco and bolted toward Joun's nest. Meanwhile, Vasco dashed off.

11

The Smell

Nighttime was already well under way. Vasco had to hurry if he wanted to hunt.

But the more he ran, the more he felt a deep sadness within him. When he'd joined Nil's tribe, Vasco had refused to think of his former life. But Coben was right: he could not forget what had happened to his mother, brothers, or the other members of his tribe.

Abruptly Vasco changed direction. He hurried through the underground network of sewers that headed north, toward the harbor.

His sense of smell did not fail him. After a long trip along the pipes, Vasco went upward. When he came out of the storm drain, he found himself right in front of the first dock of the harbor. The familiar smell of salt and oxidized metal filled his nostrils. He felt alive again. With quicksilver speed, he dashed across the wharf.

Then he raced across an asphalted area and found himself face to face with a group of rats. There were about twenty. They were unfriendly, and in a second they surrounded him. Vasco stopped and curled into a ball. He waited as he had learned to do, watching to better gauge his adversaries.

One of them stepped forward, his back arched. Vasco held his breath.

The rat ground his teeth.

Vasco ground his own even louder.

The rat hissed.

Vasco hissed even more sharply.

Silence hovered over the assembly. Having failed to dissuade his enemy, Vasco was prepared to fight, as he did every night.

But a groan broke the silence and a beige rat suddenly appeared.

"Leave him alone, Darf! I know this rat!"

"Regus!" Darf said, all the while keeping his eyes on Vasco.

Vasco got up. Yes, it was Regus, all right. He was relieved.

Speaking to the leader of the harbor rats, Regus added, "Allow us to leave!"

Darf squeaked, and at his signal all the rats regrouped behind him. They spread out quickly and disappeared behind the cranes and recently unloaded containers.

"Thanks, friend," Vasco said. "But, you know, I was ready to take him on."

"I know," Regus said. "I just wanted to save Darf's life!" Then he added, "I was looking for you, anyway. Come."

He led Vasco to the industrial district at the end of the harbor, at the tip of the peninsula. It was a deserted place. Buildings rose in the middle of fallow land that was littered with rusted casks, skeletons of cars, and burnt tires. The chemicals that had been dumped there turned the muddy earth weird colors when it rained. Only human outcasts and rats lived here, far from town. The humans had built some sheds. In the dark, it was easy to make out their crooked shapes here and there. As for the rats in the area, they prudently hid underground, coming out to eat even the most toxic trash.

Vasco's throat tightened with anguish as he entered this remote area. When his tribe had been alive, rumors had circulated that the rats who lived here suffered from strange illnesses. Their limbs were said to be deformed, their fur falling out, and their behavior unpredictable.

At the extremity of a field covered with burnt trash, Regus climbed over an embankment. Vasco caught up with him at the top and touched his companion with his whiskers. Regus registered Vasco's fear, but that did not stop him. In a few strides he was at the bottom of the embankment, slipping through the chain-link fence that enclosed the field. Vasco had no choice other than to follow him.

Both rats were now moving fast between the ruts of a path that appeared to head nowhere. Along the way, high weeds, seemingly frozen under a thick coat of salt brought by the winds, looked like snow-covered trees. The rats moved along to the rhythm of distant clanging sounds.

Eventually Regus stopped and turned to Vasco. "Several tribes have disappeared under strange circumstances," he said.

Vasco caught his breath. He rubbed his snout with his front paws. Something in the air stung his skin. It was probably the salt. He tried to focus and to understand what Regus had just said.

"What circumstances?" he asked.

"The smell," Regus said. "In the nests deserted by the tribes of the harbor, there was a smell. The same smell each time."

He led Vasco to the limits of the industrial zone, toward the piers that protected the land from high tides.

There Vasco caught sight of a wide building that stood out disquietingly against the dark sky.

12

Mystery in the Industrial Zone

"I discovered this place when I followed a truck that had the same smell as the burrows rats disappear from," said Regus. "I saw it go into that building."

"I don't see any trucks," Vasco objected, almost to reassure himself.

"They've been parked for a while," Regus explained. "The night is almost over."

Jolted by Regus' last words, Vasco remembered that he had yet to find the food he was expected to bring back to the burrow.

"I have to go!" he said, and took off.

"Wait!" Regus shouted. He caught up with Vasco and blocked his path. "Your tribe disappeared. Others have encountered the same fate. Don't you want to know why?"

Vasco began to shake nervously. He tried to sidestep Regus, but the beige rat stood his ground. A terrible anguish knotted Vasco's stomach. Everything began to blur in his head: the young ones, Memona, the mysterious message she had uttered on the harbor, and then Nil and the others. But more than anything else, Vasco saw Akar's horrible face. Vasco didn't know where his duty lay anymore—whether it was to find food in exchange for shelter or to find out why his tribe had disappeared.

Regus seemed to understand Vasco's dilemma. He sniffed Vasco's chest.

"You stink with fear," he said. "Akar makes you pay a high price for his protection!"

Vasco hung his head in shame.

"I know Akar only too well to make fun of you," Regus added seriously.

Vasco looked up. Had Regus also had problems with Akar? He was about to ask when Regus took a few leaps ahead.

"I'll help you bring back some food," the beige rat declared. "In return, promise to come back here tomorrow before sunset."

Vasco looked toward the long, dark building. Of course he wanted to find out the truth. Tomorrow, when the harbor waters took on their rosy evening color, he would return.

The two rats hurried along the dirt path, slid under the fence, jumped over the embankment, and crossed the industrial zone. Vasco sensed a rebirth within him—a desire to understand and to live his life. He was determined not to allow his behavior to be dictated by Akar's orders. His role in the world of rats would not be limited to fattening Ourga.

13

Vasco's Revolt

When Vasco finally reached the burrow, the dominant females were headed to the communal room for their nightly feast. Those who had given birth during the night were lying on their flanks, offering their nipples to babies who clung to them clumsily. Strong odors of urine, droppings, flesh, and blood invaded each nook of the nest. This smell would never be his. He might live here now, but in the folds of his fur, he would always retain the scents of iodine and rust, as did all the rats of the harbor.

Yet Vasco respected the terms of his deal with Akar.

He dragged the piece of meat that he had found with Regus' help and deposited it in the room where Akar and Ourga were waiting for him.

When he entered, his nostrils quivered under the assault of smells. It seemed as if the contents of an entire garbage can had been emptied in the center of the room. These included vegetable peels, bread crusts, cheese rinds, rice grains, french fries, a burnt tomato, and the carcass of a chicken, along with various wrappings that no rat, even a well-fed one, refused to gnaw at.

Hunger tormented Vasco but he knew that he was not authorized to help himself. He approached Ourga and deposited the piece of meat under her nose. The fat female uttered a satisfied sound. The meat, covered with a greenish mold, was a choice piece. It was big enough to satisfy the appetite of a dozen rats.

Right away Akar approached his female and tore away with his teeth at the plastic wrapping of the meat. Both rats dug their snouts in the flesh. Their jaws moved in rhythm, their teeth cutting, slicing, and grinding. Soon their tummies bulged.

The families of second-ranking rats gathered at the entrance of the room, hungry but resigned. They waited their turn in silence. Akar and Ourga continued to gorge themselves. Their voracity knew no limit.

At the sight of such greed, Vasco felt an uncontrollable

rage surge within him. He could no longer contain his anger and bolted onto his hind legs.

"You're a monster, Akar!" he shouted.

Akar and Ourga stopped gnawing.

"You feed the anger of your own people by starving them!" Vasco went on.

Akar swallowed noisily and circled the piece of meat as he approached Vasco. Already his hunters had gathered, ready to intervene.

A shudder went through the crowd.

Lek and Joun were hiding in the shadows. Looking worried, Nil came out of the ranks to be closer to the confrontation. Tension increased as Akar began to grind his teeth.

Vasco answered with a hiss. The fur on his back bristled. Akar took a step closer. He released a spurt of urine, the ultimate signal to convince an adversary to give up. But Vasco clicked his teeth as noisily as he could. He wasn't backing down.

Both rats were now close to each other, each at a standstill, when an unexpected stir disconcerted Akar. Nil had come to stand by Vasco's side.

The hunters moved forward and flanked Ourga, ready to jump. The female swished her tail and spat to incite Akar to fight.

In Vasco's mind, everything was clear. He was

determined to do battle. To maintain his courage, he thought of Regus, of the harbor, of Memona and how her body had fallen from the wharf into the water. A wave of outrage invaded him.

Then to everyone's surprise, Lek emerged from his dark corner. The skinny and frail rat crossed the room, his head high, and joined Nil and Vasco.

"Go back to your place, Lek!" Akar thundered.

Lek ignored him. Worse still, Joun and her young ones came forward as well and enlarged the line of rebels.

"Our place is with Vasco," Lek said. "After Lod's death, we behaved in a cowardly manner and let you take control, Akar. When you fought with . . . with the rat who wanted to oppose you, we should have helped him. But none of us did and you killed him. Enough is enough."

A murmur spread through the assembly. Lek's reference to Akar's past fight made the huge rat shudder. Now Vasco understood why Akar limped.

"I don't know who made a cripple of you," Vasco shouted. "But believe me, I won't let you live."

The whole tribe grew agitated at these words. Some moved forward to swell the line of hunters faithful to Akar. About thirty others joined the mutineers. In a few seconds, what was to have been a regular fight looked like it was about to become an all-out war.

Vasco and Akar stood still. The war would begin when one of them pounced on the other. But Vasco refused to be responsible for such a bloodbath. The rats on his side were feeble. They were facing the best-fed and strongest rats. The slaughter had to be avoided at all costs.

"Allow us to leave!" Vasco said suddenly.

Akar snarled hatefully.

"We'll go and settle far from your territory. Let us leave," Vasco repeated.

Behind him, the mutineers silently agreed. They were ready to abandon the burrow and to follow this courageous rat.

Just then Akar sprang forward. Vasco quickly moved aside, narrowly dodging the attack.

"Run!" he shouted to those who had joined ranks with him.

14

The Fugitives

Thirty or forty rats rushed toward the narrow opening of the burrow—adult rats, young rats, and frightened infants who hung on to their mother's nipples, fur, and tail. The thundering noise of their flight was matched by the enraged cries of those chasing them.

Vasco pushed his group in front of him in the dark. "To the sewers! Quickly!" he shouted.

The rats crossed the hole and ran along the underground corridor. Once they arrived at the copper sheet, they tumbled on top of and trampled each other, hurting themselves against the obstacle.

One at a time will be too slow, Vasco thought.

He forced his way through the pile of bodies and started gnawing at the copper sheet. The strongest males also attacked the metal with their teeth. Together they managed to enlarge the opening just as Akar and his hunters swooped down on them.

Lek pushed the females and young ones out in front. A few males at the rear tried to hold off the pursuers. Vasco threw himself into the fray. He grabbed the throat of a hunter and bit him with all his strength. The taste of blood flooded his mouth. He tightened his grip and shook his head from side to side. His adversary fell dead.

Several of his companions collapsed under the relentless scratching and biting. Vasco felt the corpses piling under his paws. He wasn't thinking anymore. He jumped ahead in the dark and bit another hunter in the face as the two of them tumbled in the dirt.

Suddenly one of Vasco's companions, an old bald rat, shouted, "Take off, Vasco! Go with the others before it's too late!"

Vasco refused. "I won't abandon you! We have to win together!"

"Go, I'm telling you!" the old rat insisted. "We'll slow them down as much as we can. If you stay, all of us are done for."

Vasco thought about the ones who were ahead, those who were alive: Lek, Joun, Nil, Tiel, Hog, Coben, and the others. They were relying on him; the old rat was right.

As he retreated, a rat bit down on his tail fiercely. After a struggle Vasco freed himself and jumped out of the hole. He knew that a tailless rat could not maintain his balance—he had just escaped a terrible fate. He ran, dizzy and weary, leaving the battleground behind him.

It didn't take him long to catch up to Lek and to take the group under his command. But the deeper they went into the tunnels, the more Vasco doubted that this was the right solution. Akar and his hunters knew the sewers well. It wouldn't be long before they caught up with the fugitives.

So Vasco stopped. Heading upward was the way to go. Only on the outside could Vasco hope to lose Akar.

On his signal, the group turned around.

In the middle of a main sewer was a junction that Vasco had passed several times before. He hugged the walls until he found the corridor that led to the surface. The rats climbed over old mattresses soaked with water and all matter of filth, over piles of rusted cans and shapeless objects glued together by mud, before they reached a shaft at the end of which appeared a circle of light.

"Climb quickly!" Vasco ordered as he heard the shouts of their pursuers in the main sewer.

He helped the youngest to scale the rough cement.

Above, Lek caught them between his teeth and sent them up toward the light.

There was no time to waste. Vasco intensified his effort. When he finally climbed up to meet the others, Akar's hunters were closing in.

Vasco rallied his troop. Nil was exhausted. Her fur was plastered on her belly. But in spite of everything, she looked at Vasco with gratitude.

"This way," he ordered.

Gingerly, the fugitives stuck their heads through the grate. They had eluded Akar; now they would have to confront the world of men.

On the sidewalk, the crowd was hurrying under umbrellas. Speeding cars sent splashes of water up over the curb. And now the loud purring of an engine attracted Vasco's attention. A street sweeper was moving in their direction, its huge rotating brooms cleaning the gutter.

Vasco signaled to the others to be on the ready.

The purring came closer. They could hear the grating of the brooms against the asphalt. Right when the noise was at its loudest, Vasco gave the signal. All the rats sprang from the storm drain and found themselves under the truck.

They progressed this way for a while, protected by the huge machine, until Vasco spotted a backyard where debris had piled up. Now was the time.

Vasco leaped and all the others followed.

Within seconds, they reached the pile of rubbish—a huge concrete mound of gypsum board and iron railings, obviously the remains of a demolition site.

Vasco, Lek, and Nil sniffed each crack. It was cold and there was no food around, but no alien colony had set up camp here.

"It will give us shelter," Lek said approvingly.

Right away the females went in search of tidbits to build their nests. *All this will probably be temporary,* Vasco thought. But as he watched the young ones run around the iron railings, he felt satisfaction at having saved them.

● ● ●

Night was about to fall. Lek volunteered to go hunting. Vasco didn't feel right about this, but he remembered his appointment with Regus on the harbor. He didn't know what to do.

"Go," Nil told him. "We're safe here! We'll manage."

15

The Truck

When he reached the harbor, Vasco detected Regus' scent and followed it to the warehouse. He saw a few rats busying themselves around a ripped-up crate. It held a load of bananas that had probably fallen off a crane and that men had not bothered to pick up. Regus was among the guests.

The harbor rats stopped their feast to size up Vasco. Upon recognizing him, they went back to their bananas. His whiskers covered with pulp, Regus pushed a fruit toward Vasco.

To eat! What a joy! Vasco grabbed the fruit, tore at it, and swallowed it, skin included. He did not mention the events of the evening, nor his escape, nor his confrontation with Akar. For the time being, he preferred not to think about those he had left on the pile of debris.

Once he had eaten his fill, he signaled to Regus that he was ready.

Both rats left the surroundings of the warehouse. Without a word, they ran to the industrial zone, up to the building where the trucks were hidden.

It was night. A light, cold rain insinuated itself into their fur.

Suddenly a door opened and the imposing mass of a truck moved forward, its lights off. Hidden in the grass, the two rats waited. Then they bounded out of their hiding place and jumped onto the step at the back of the vehicle.

The jouncing of the truck tossed them about, but they managed to climb higher and grab a rubber hose by their teeth. The driver made his way toward a paved road, turned his headlights on, and accelerated. Vasco and Regus hung on tight. Through the curtain of rain that veiled the landscape, they saw the lights of the harbor pass by, the dark skeletons of the loading cranes, and the smokestacks of the cargo ships.

The truck entered the town through a residential area. Elegant apartment buildings and big townhouses hugged one another behind a line of trees. Eventually the vehicle stopped in front of a red brick building.

Vasco and Regus slipped under the chassis, gasping for air. They were scared. Men dressed in overalls and wearing gloves got out of the cab of the truck and headed to the rear of the vehicle. They started a motor and dragged the rubber hose inside the building. A few seconds later, a loud signal was heard. The hose inflated. The machine sent out hissing sounds.

"Can you smell that?" Regus whispered.

In the dark, Vasco nodded gravely. His whiskers quivered as he sniffed, trying to think of what this odor could possibly be. It was unlike anything he was familiar with. It didn't bring to mind a sense of danger or food; the odor was totally new. Worst of all, it was not unpleasant.

A commotion at the entrance of the building attracted their attention. The men were exiting the building, walking backward as they pulled on the hose. They moved slowly and with care, like fishermen pulling on a net heavy with fish.

Vasco stepped forward for a better view. Something black was moving on the ground, right at the men's feet. It seemed to be spreading like a liquid. Taking another step forward, Vasco soon realized that the spreading black stain was none other than a swarm of rats—a tide of black fur that had erupted from the basement.

Terrorized, Vasco hurried back under the wheels of

the truck. He huddled by Regus' side. The closer the men came, the stronger was the smell.

"Don't breathe in!" Vasco shouted.

Regus nodded. "We have to go," he said.

But the odor seemed to work like a magnet on their sense of smell. Their limbs grew numb. It took an immense effort for them not to rush toward the truck like the other rats. Instead they crawled in the opposite direction, and in a burst of energy they ran off along the sidewalk.

A man yelled as he saw them. Shouts exploded behind them. But Vasco and Regus ran without looking back, breathing in deeply the humid air of the night. When they reached the end of the street, they slowed down and tried to regain their composure.

Vasco turned just in time to see the last rats rush into the open tub at the rear of the truck. A few seconds later, the doors slammed shut and the truck started up, leaving only the silence of the night behind it.

Vasco shuddered. He remembered Memona's last words.

"Be cautious of men. Of the steam," he said out loud.

16

Regus Among His Own

Vasco shook his numb legs. He felt as if he were coming out of a daze. Next to him, Regus stretched his back muscles. Suddenly they heard meows in the distance.

"Follow me!" Vasco said.

The two rats slipped along the streets, between the parked cars. They left excrement behind them as a warning to their fellow rats that the area was dangerous.

Vasco had a hard time finding his bearings. His snout in the air, he looked for the way to the pile of trash, the way to his new burrow. Regus followed him like a sleepwalker. Vasco wandered for a bit but found his way at last. The demolition site was in front of them, protected by a simple chain-link fence. A rusted panel warned humans of danger. But where humans didn't venture, rats moved in.

Vasco stopped a few steps away from the collapsed concrete debris.

"We've left Akar's tribe," Vasco explained to Regus. "Me and some others. This is our shelter."

Regus shook himself and got up on his legs. "I've seen more comfortable burrows," he declared, taking hold of the fence. "But it's not that bad for a novice."

Vasco expected him to take off, but to his surprise Regus followed him inside. Vasco did not comment. He was worried about the others. Had they been able to feed and shelter themselves? His concerns were assuaged when he saw the young rats scamper up to him.

"Lek brought us food!" Tiel exclaimed.

"A sparrow that's hardly damaged," Coben added. "Delicious!"

Nil appeared. She froze when she noticed the presence of the stranger.

"He's a friend," Vasco reassured her.

Vasco explained to Nil what Regus had done for him. But he did not mention their adventure with the truck. He would do so later, when the whole tribe was gathered.

Once Nil accepted the stranger, all three moved to the center of the trash pile. They found Lek and Joun surrounded by their young ones and by all those who had escaped from the hunters. Lek jumped back. It was his turn to perceive the presence of an outsider. His back arched, his whiskers twitched, and his eyes tried to pierce the obscurity.

"He's with me," Vasco repeated. "You have nothing to fear, Lek."

Lek remained still, his eyes wide open. Joun and the little ones came to snuggle up against him.

"Who is this rat?" Lek asked finally. "I recognize his smell."

Vasco did not have time to answer. Regus passed in front of him and positioned himself in front of Lek.

"Regus." It was Joun who spoke the name in a faint voice.

Several males came out of the nooks and climbed over blocks of concrete to see what was happening. The females protecting their little ones only raised their heads. They listened and sniffed. They too recognized Regus' scent. Vasco and Nil did not understand what was going on.

"We thought you were dead," Lek said at last.

Immediately Vasco understood why his companion seemed to know Akar.

"It's you!" he shouted. "You who fought with Akar! You made him lame!"

"In the past, Regus was one of our tribe," Lek explained. "The older ones remember him."

Regus then turned to Vasco. "Akar and I were born of the same female," he confessed. "But let's forget all that."

Joun, Lek, and the others came closer to the beige rat. Clearly they had not forgotten that when Lod, the former chief of the tribe, had died, Regus had been the only one to oppose Akar's rise to power.

"At the end of the fight, I fell in a deep hole somewhere in the sewers," Regus said. "The others assumed I was dead. When I managed to get out, I chose to disappear and live alone."

Vasco looked at him with admiration and surprise. He now understood why his companion was so leery of Akar's tribe.

"At the time, we behaved like cowards," Lek said. "We knew of Akar's cruelty, yet we did nothing to resist him. Welcome back, Regus."

The strident noise of screeching tires reached their ears. Daybreak was several hours away, but eventually men were going to repossess the streets.

Vasco shuddered. He too had a story to tell. He climbed over an old broken sink in the middle of the debris and requested the attention of the assembly. He told them what he had seen: the truck, the hose, the tide of black rats inundating the street. He looked at Tiel, Hog, and Coben.

"This is probably how our tribe disappeared—

swallowed by a truck. We have to be even more careful than ever. If a truck stops here, we must flee." Turning toward Regus, he added, "We think the trucks take those of our race to the industrial zone. We have to find out what is happening. The fate of our kind is at stake!"

17

The Killing Machine

Night had fallen when Vasco and Regus returned to the industrial zone. A cold wind swept the streets. The humans who had homes shut themselves up behind their doors. Those who were homeless lit fires in metal barrels at the corner of alleys. Vasco and Regus carefully avoided the latter since they knew they could end up barbecued at the end of a stick.

The two rats crossed several backyards, went up and down fire escapes, and sometimes climbed up to rooftops, preferring aerial routes over the paths in the sewers. Underground, they ran the risk of meeting Akar.

As they came down along a downspout, they spotted a truck. The vehicle was stationed in front of a building, its motor running. Vasco recognized the unrolled hose at the back. He smelled the dangerous—and enticing— emanations.

Men came out of the building, pulling on the hose. In its wake, dozens of rats emerged as if hypnotized.

Regus got frightened and backed away. But Vasco knew that if he wanted to find out where the rats were headed, he had to approach the snare.

"Stay here," he shouted to Regus. "I should be the one to go!"

He left his companion and ran toward the truck. Holding his breath, he mingled with the other rats and climbed the step. In front of him, the hose rolled up on its stand. The dark mouth of the scoop opened up. Hundreds of rats rushed inside, their survival instincts having disappeared.

Vasco nearly lost his balance on the threshold of the scoop as he was pushed along by the other rats. At the last moment, he managed to climb along the hose and wedge himself in a nook. He inhaled a little, not too much, so as not to succumb to the steam that was escaping from the scoop.

During the trip, an invigorating wind allowed him to recover his presence of mind.

A squeak startled him.

"Regus!"

Regus was right above him, crouched in a fold of the hose. "Did you think I was going to let you go off by yourself?" he said.

The town passed by around them. The truck went through populated and well-lit areas. Then they reached the harbor again, and finally the bumpy path that led to the mysterious building.

Vasco felt better now. He remained hidden, his heart beating violently.

At the end of the trip, the truck rushed inside the building. The door slid shut. The motor stopped. Vasco stuck out his snout and discovered a large, dimly lit room. He looked for Regus but did not see him.

The men got out of the truck and attached a large hose at the rear that went into a room next door. The scoop creaked as it opened. Vasco leaned forward. He could hear squeaks and trampling noises as the rats left the scoop. The hose shook. Then nothing . . .

At that moment Vasco felt something grab his neck. A man had caught him! He tried to free himself but could not. He turned his head to bite the hand that held him, but his teeth were unable to go through the man's thick glove. The man tightened his grip. He lifted Vasco and carried him to a large metal cage, where he threw him among the other rats.

Vasco felt the almost lifeless bodies of his wretched companions under his paws. Males, females, young ones . . . they were warm and alive but put up no struggle.

Where was Regus? Vasco sniffed and looked for him in vain.

Meanwhile, outside the cage, men were busy working on a huge machine. Buttons were lit and flashed as they pushed on them. A long transparent tunnel went around the machine like a belt.

Suddenly the lights of the machine stopped blinking. A blowing engine started. The men stood still. Something was happening. Fear invaded Vasco. Around him, the other rats did not react.

With a click, a door opened at the end of the cage. Vasco felt the ground give way under his paws. He was on a conveyor belt. The rats closer to the door slipped to the other side and into the transparent tunnel. Then the conveyor stopped and the door shut. Through the bars of the cage, Vasco saw the rats move forward in the tunnel. Those who still had enough strength to react skidded along the smooth surface, looking aghast.

Men threw the machine into gear. Lightning swirled through the tunnel. It lasted a split second. Those rats who were trapped no longer walked, skidded, or even moved. They simply lay at the bottom, dead stiff.

18

The Great Threat

Without a cry or call, the rats died unknowingly. They hadn't even been able to warn their own of the danger. Vasco was terrified; he understood that this device was the most formidable that men had ever engineered. If rats couldn't warn each other, their entire species was threatened.

Vasco moved as far away as he could from the door, which was opening again. The conveyor belt ran under the paws of more rats, and about a hundred of them were sent to the tunnel. The same thing happened—lightning struck the rats, the door reopened, and the conveyor belt moved forward. Each time Vasco went deeper into the cage. But what was the use? Soon he wouldn't be able to retreat any farther. He would be the last one to die. But he would put up a fight and the men would notice that he fought back and they would throw him in the tunnel. That would be his end.

No! Vasco thought, determined to find a solution.

As he observed the tunnel, he noticed an opening in its transparent wall. Men put their hands through it to make sure that the door was properly closed. To reach that opening, Vasco would have to let himself glide onto the conveyor belt.

He joined the rats dazed by the steam and waited for the next grouping.

Briskly, the door opened in front of him and the conveyor took him to the other side. Vasco raised his head. Now was the time! He leaped through the other opening.

When he landed on the ground, the men started shouting. At that moment, Regus appeared from his hiding place right behind the machine and jumped on the ground at the same time as Vasco. The men were too surprised to react quickly enough.

Vasco scrambled under the truck. Regus headed the other way.

Vasco let out a high-pitched squeal. Regus answered.

Both of them ran across the garage, changing direction constantly. Vasco scurried, stopped, curled up, zigzagged, and slipped between the legs of his pursuers.

Meanwhile Regus climbed over a shelf and knocked down metal boxes. Right away, Vasco jumped on the other side.

Armed with shovels and brooms, the men struck at random, without reaching their target.

Now Vasco heard the noise of an engine. A truck was starting.

"Careful, Regus, the steam!" he shouted.

Regus sped down the shelf and fled toward a pile of crates. They heard the sound of a second engine. *I can't believe it!* Vasco thought. *Do men need two trucks to get rid of us?*

But the door of the garage opened suddenly and the cold night air drifted into the room. The men were shouting furiously. Vasco did not try to understand this miracle. He came out of the nook where he was hiding. Regus leaped behind him. Together they rushed outside.

They barely avoided the wheels of a vehicle parked in front of the door. The second engine was that of another truck coming back to the garage. The driver was startled by the commotion inside.

The two rats didn't linger. They fled into the night, zigzagging until they reached the end of the industrial zone. They stopped only long enough to catch their breath before moving on again across the empty lots that bordered the harbor.

When they approached a residential area, Vasco and Regus slowed down. Dazed and disoriented, they made their way under the hedges of well-kept gardens, walked around ponds, and finally reached a large and quiet street.

Vasco was worried. There was something abnormal in the air—a sinister silence, an odor of desolation. Dead leaves swirled in a gust of wind.

Suddenly Regus called out. There was no answer. He turned toward Vasco. His eyes were filled with terror. In the basements, in the garbage cans, in the backyards, in the nooks of the street . . . there was not a rat in sight. None had answered his call.

"They're all dead," Regus murmured.

Vasco shuddered. The area had been completely cleansed of his kind. Here men had won the battle. They had found a way to free the town of its rats!

"The others! We have to warn them!" Vasco said.

"It may already be too late," Regus answered grimly.

The two rats left the area and made their way to Vasco's shelter. As they approached the pile of debris, Vasco wondered again if his tribe had disappeared in this gruesome way.

19

Rendezvous at the Harbor

In the burrow, Vasco and Regus were met by frightened squeaks. Nil, Joun, and the young ones retreated toward the back before they recognized who had entered.

"Vasco!" Nil cried. "What's going on?"

Vasco looked at his companions as if they were ghosts. A sour smell wafted from him. He was out of breath and his eyes shone with an unusual intensity.

Joun instinctively hid the young ones behind her. Vasco's attitude brought back an ancestral fear. His eyes, his smell, his breath . . .

"You're ill, Vasco," Joun said.

Her words snapped Vasco out of his torpor. He realized that the rats in front of him were very much alive. His breathing returned to normal and he rubbed his snout to get rid of the morbid odor that had impregnated his fur.

"No, I'm not ill," he murmured.

But he was worn out and unable to explain what had happened. So Regus spoke for him. He described the sinister building of the industrial zone, the truck, and the steam that had paralyzed the rats' willpower. Then he told them of the existence of the killing machine. The rats listened, their eyes filled with terror.

"We have no choice," Vasco cut in. "We must leave town."

"But Regus says that the trucks are everywhere," Lek dared to object. "If we leave, they'll get us too."

Vasco looked down in silence. There was only one way out—the harbor.

"The ships!" he said. "The ships are our only means of escape. We have to embark tonight."

Vasco's eyes met Nil's forlorn gaze. The young female seemed to reject the idea of fleeing. She turned in circles, indecisive.

"I can't leave without warning my tribe," she said. "I have to speak to Akar."

"No!" shouted Vasco. "We don't have time!"

Nil went up on her hind legs. "If you'd been able to save your tribe, you would have done so without hesitation," she said firmly. "I have to do what's right."

Vasco did not have time to answer before Nil ran out of the burrow.

"Wait!" Vasco shouted.

But Nil was already in the street and kept going without looking back. Vasco made a move in her direction but stopped. He looked at Tiel, Hog, and Coben, who were trembling, pressed against one another. Time was of the essence. If he did not take them directly to the harbor, they would die. All of them would.

Regus appraoched Vasco. "You stay here!" he said. "I'll go after Nil."

"If Akar learns that you're alive, he'll kill you," Lek spoke up in a shaky voice.

"But he may also kill Nil," Regus answered back.

Vasco was at a loss. His thoughts were confused.

"Let me go," Regus insisted. "We'll meet you at the harbor."

Vasco looked at his friend and nodded. "Rendezvous at the harbor," he said.

Wasting no time, Regus left the burrow. Vasco knew that Nil had a good lead; Regus would have to hurry.

20

Underground Chaos

Regus followed the scent marks to his former nest. His whiskers touched the oozing walls of the underground sewers, helping to guide him in the dark. He was reunited with the stench, the warm and noxious inhalations of the pipes. He jumped from one bridge to another, went down along drains, always heading farther below. When he reached the larger drain, he could hear squeaks. His heart jumped. He slowed, his ears pricking up. The noise was coming closer, and it sounded like hundreds of paws scratching the concrete.

Regus moved toward the canal. A group of frightened rats emerged right in front.

There were so many that they invaded the whole width of the cornice. Some jumped in the water and swam; others ran straight ahead in the same sense of panic. Regus could feel his fur bristle; if he stayed here, he was going to be trampled. He turned around and started to run. The swarming troop was gaining on him.

At the last second, Regus found a nook in the wall. He rushed in and made himself small. All he could do was watch as hundreds of rats made a mad and deafening dash toward parts unknown. Regus had never witnessed such chaos. Were the men already in the sewers? And Nil? Regus could not believe that she had gotten caught by surprise. For the first time in a long while, he feared for another rat.

Finally the tumult ended. A strange silence hovered in the sewers. Regus came out of his hiding spot. The area was deserted. Even the insects that usually crowded the walls were gone. He moved forward again, going across narrowing inlets until he found the main concrete drain. His nose quivered as he went up toward the building and walked over the copper sheet, which now lay flat on the ground.

When he reached the hole, Regus caught his breath and was on the alert for smells and noises from the nest.

He did not pick up Nil's scent, only that of blood and pu-trefied vegetables.

Trying to control his shaking legs, Regus prepared to enter the long corridor. If Akar was still there, he would confront him. And surely one of them would die once and for all.

21

Vasco's Mission

Vasco stood on his hind legs and raised his snout to the sky. Familiar smells of salt, fish, rust, and burnt rubber filled his nostrils. Here, on the harbor, nothing seemed to have changed. He almost believed that life was as it had been in the past. But the reality was different. Over at the end of the peninsula, the wide building was visible. And men were busy with their work of destruction.

Behind Vasco, the young ones were playing in the middle of an empty lot. They gnawed at an old sandal and ran around logs. Hog and Tiel led the game under the attentive eyes of the females. Everything seemed normal, quiet, almost happy. But all the rats were waiting for Vasco's signal.

Gradually twilight arrived and rain clouds gathered over the ocean. The foghorn sounded in the harbor as the cranes slowly turned on their stands. Vasco watched the men's doings. Several freighters seemed ready to get under way. But where were Nil and Regus?

"What about hiding here and waiting until tomorrow?" suggested Lek, who sensed Vasco's anxiety.

Vasco shook his head. They couldn't wait that long.

Night had come. All of Vasco's senses were alert. He had succeeded in leading his group to this vacant lot behind the harbor. Now he had to guide them to the loading dock. He sent out a cry. The young ones stopped their games and joined the females.

Vasco took the lead, and in a long, silent file they made their way over the railroad tracks. They hurried. The females grabbed the youngest ones between their teeth to help them clear the most difficult obstacles. Soon they gathered behind the first warehouse. Vasco ordered a break. He sniffed the paving stones, hesitated, then circled a container. Waxy cubes, half gnawed, were set at the corners. A strong smell of urine and excrement signaled that the cubes were poisoned lures. The message was transmitted: no other rat would touch them. A few steps away, Vasco recognized the scent he was looking for—Darf's scent.

Vasco kept his nose to the ground and led his group to the second warehouse. In front of the door, under the clear light of projectors, men were busying themselves around huge bundles of goods. They shouted at each other and manipulated chains and pulleys. Going in that direction was out of the question.

Vasco was about to turn around when he heard the squeaks. While the females were busy with the babies, several young rats had rushed toward crates piled up at the back of the warehouse. Vasco knew that the slightest foolish act would spoil everything. He ran toward them, followed by the rest of the group.

"Come and see!" Tiel called.

At the bottom of the crates lay the corpses of several rats. The young ones sniffed at them, curious and puzzled. Vasco moved forward and distributed a few blows to scatter the little ones. He touched one of the lifeless bodies with the tips of his whiskers.

"Darf," he whispered.

The dominant rat of the harbor lay on his side, his head angled back. No wound was visible on his body but it sent out that dull smell that accompanies death. Between Darf's teeth, Vasco could see small pieces of the poisoned lures. Darf and some members of his tribe had no doubt been hungry and careless enough to gnaw at them. But they had had the strength to urinate all around the crates when they understood that they were about to die.

Vasco looked to his own. "Come," he told them. "Hurry!"

At full speed, the group slipped behind the warehouse and reached a deserted wharf where a freighter was moored. The gangplanks had been removed and the crew was already on board.

22

Enemy Brothers

Akar had detected Nil's presence. He sniffed and sent out a muted cry, his impressive frame towering above the group of rats gathered in the communal room. Nil knew that she could not retreat. She was terrified at the sight of her former chief, but it was for the others—the females and the young ones—that she wanted to speak. So she lay down low, her snout on the ground, and crawled toward Akar.

A few centimeters from the chief, she stopped and raised her head. All the eyes of the tribe were on her.

"I was hoping you were dead," Akar said. "That's what traitors like you deserve!"

Nil's throat was tight, jammed with fear. Akar came close to sniff at her.

"What are you doing here?" he asked menacingly.

The young female took a deep breath. "I—I came to warn you. You must leave the city."

Right away, the group of rats grew agitated. They began to squeak, groan, and spit.

"It's the men," Nil went on. "They're exterminating—"

The scratching blow was quick. A trickle of blood appeared on Nil's fur. She cried in pain. Another blow hit her on the head.

"This is *my* warning!" Akar growled.

For the first time Nil smelled her own blood. Frightened, she crawled back.

"Get out! Or I'll kill you," Akar warned.

Nil stood up. "Don't stay here!" she shouted to the tribe. "Men have already killed half the rats in the city!"

Akar was so enraged he jumped on her and bit her cruelly. Nil struggled and escaped. She gathered what was left of her strength and ran along the underground corridor. Akar chased her, encouraged by Ourga's cries.

Just as Nil reached the hole, Akar was on top of her, his mouth full of drool and his eyes gleaming with hatred.

She could feel his claws enter her flanks, and she collapsed. Nil closed her eyes as she waited for the fatal blow.

But Akar let out a cry. A rat had thrown himself at him and bitten his back.

Nil stood up again. The rat let Akar go and came to her side, in a fighting position. Akar seemed wounded. He turned to his opponent, dumbfounded.

"Regus . . . ," he said at last.

Courage returned to Nil and she huddled close to her savior. "You didn't kill him!" she told Akar. "Regus is alive."

"Let us go, Akar!" Regus spoke up. "All it would take is for the others to see me and your authority would vanish. I'm not dead. You took power but you did not deserve it!"

Akar's eyes filled with anger again. He swished his tail and scratched the ground.

"I made you lame during our last fight!" Regus reminded him. "This time I'll slaughter you."

Nil raised herself beside him. She felt ready to fight to the bitter end.

Noises and squeals came from the burrow. Akar turned toward the nest. The tribe was coming. The rats wanted to see what was going on.

Akar took a few steps back, grinding his teeth. This time he was the one who was afraid.

"I'll find you again," he murmured to Regus in a last burst of pride. Then he turned and disappeared into the corridor of the burrow.

"Quick!" said Regus. "The others are waiting for us."

When Regus and Nil reached the concrete slab, Nil stopped, out of breath. Regus sniffed at her. His whiskers quivered. He discovered the wound on Nil's side and licked it clean.

Nil finally stood up and shook herself.

"Come," said Regus. "Vasco is already at the harbor."

23

Clandestine Boarding

Vasco explored the wharf, sniffing the air, attentive to the slightest noise. Reassured, he signaled to his companions to follow him. Steel cables stretched between the dock and the freighter. One by one they would have to make their way across as cautiously as possible. Vasco ordered Lek to go first.

Lek climbed on the cable without hesitation, using his tail to balance himself. He moved rapidly toward the hull and disappeared through an opening. He had done it: Lek was on board.

On the dock, Vasco pushed a female up. The young one she was holding between her teeth threw off her balance and she wasn't moving fast. But time was of the essence, and before she even reached the ship, Vasco sent a male up. Then another female, a young rat, a male . . . At least thirty rats filed across in this fashion. Then Tiel, Coben, and Hog dashed one after the other, following Joun. when they had all disappeared inside the freighter, Vasco was immensely relieved.

Only one female remained, the one who was expecting. She hesitated; her belly was so heavy that she was afraid of falling. Vasco accompanied her along the cable. Two-thirds of the way, he let her continue alone and came back down. As long as the freighter was moored, Vasco would not climb aboard. He would wait for Nil and Regus.

But ripples soon appeared in the water around the hull of the freighter. The engines rumbled. Vasco saw a tugboat pass by, then another. Up in the pilot's cabin, the light was turned on. Departure was imminent.

24

Departure Toward the Unknown

Nil and Regus made their way across town again. They encountered a few lost rats in the streets and saw furtive shadows in hiding or fleeing an impalpable danger. The areas where the trucks had already done their work were enveloped in silence. Soon the entire population of rats would disappear from the city. Men would win the war they had waged for such a long time.

At last the two rats reached the harbor. Nil tripped on the uneven paving stones, while Regus sniffed the ground and followed Vasco's scent. The smell of females and young rats indicated that most of the group had passed this way. And suddenly, he could see Vasco on the very edge of the wharf, standing on his hind legs.

• • •

When he spotted his two companions, Vasco sighed, deeply relieved. The wait had been unbearable. Several times he'd thought they would never come and that he would have to leave without them.

Vasco touched Nil's whiskers. "And Akar?" he asked.

"I tried to warn him!" Nil answered. "He wouldn't listen to me. Regus showed him who was the strongest."

"The others are on board," Vasco explained. "The freighter is about to leave."

He could see that Nil was exhausted, but he pushed her toward the mooring.

"I won't make it," she whispered, looking at the steep slope of the cable.

"You will!" Regus told her. "Get going."

Breathing fast, the young female placed her paws on the cable. The narrow path was hardly visible in the dark. She moved ahead a little, then stopped. The dark water danced beneath her. Regus and Vasco called out to her encouragingly, and she took a few more steps. The cable was now angled almost vertically. This didn't usually hamper a rat, but Nil was worn out.

"Go help her!" Regus told Vasco.

Vasco climbed the cable. Before he disappeared in the darkness, he turned to Regus.

"Come with me!"

Regus did not move.

"Come!" Vasco repeated.

Suddenly Nil squeaked in panic. Vasco pricked up his ears and rushed over to where the sound was coming from. Nil squeaked again. He found that she had slipped and was hanging on to the cable with her front legs, her body suspended in the void.

Vasco leaned down and grabbed Nil by the skin of her back. His teeth firmly set in her fur, he pulled with all his strength. Nil came up gradually. At last all her paws were on the cable again.

Both rats climbed together toward the freighter. At the end, Nil rushed through the opening. The squeaks coming from inside signaled to Vasco that everything was fine.

The engines of the freighter were turning at full speed now. A phosphorescent froth whirled above the propellers. Vasco could hear men giving orders on the deck. Others were busy on the dock. Beams of light scoured the wharf. The cables would soon be drawn up, and Regus would no longer be able to join them.

Vasco hesitated to jump onto the freighter. He didn't dare come down again, but he didn't want to go aboard either. He stood frozen, the void under him. In the distance, the town was all lit. A cold wind was rising.

Vasco thought he could see rats scurrying toward the ship. But no, those were only shadows. Vasco was so tired that he was no longer certain whether he was alive. He felt as if he were floating in the air, above the sea, above the harbor and the city. It was an unreal sensation.

Suddenly he felt the cable slip under his paws. He clung to it and cried out. Without thinking, he climbed. He had no choice now. He entered through the hole and jumped onto a ledge. Lek and Nil were waiting for him.

"Where's Regus?" Lek asked anxiously.

Vasco turned to look. At that instant, Regus' whiskers appeared through the hole and the beige rat jumped down breathlessly next to Nil. He had made it. Behind him, the cable creaked and coiled around its winch. The freighter was leaving port.

"Come," Lek said. "The females found a quiet nook. Let's follow their scent."

Regus, Nil, and Vasco followed without a word. A dull sound from the engines indicated that the tugboats were guiding the freighter out of the harbor . . . out to where the vast ocean lay before them, as well as an adventure into the complete unknown.

His heart beating furiously, Vasco looked at his three companions. Were they aware that they had become fugitives and stowaways? Had they pondered the dangers that awaited them? Vasco shuddered. What counted now, most of all, was that they form a real tribe.

**IN THE EYE
OF THE STORM**

1

Locked In

Vasco stopped in the center of the hold. His nostrils quivered as he raised himself slightly on his hind legs, his senses alert. He was surrounded by darkness. The damp cold seeped through his fur, numbing his muscles.

Cold, dampness, darkness, and hunger—that was what he and his companions had found on the freighter.

For several days Vasco had been plagued by a haunting question: how could he have allowed the tribe to fall into such a trap? He should have known better. But he had been so tired that he had followed Lek without thinking.

The quiet nook that the females had discovered turned out to be a double-locked hold—a dead end. The rats had tumbled into it one after the other after passing through an air vent. As soon as they understood that they were trapped inside, it was too late. The air vent was now out of reach, high up above a metal wall that offered no grip. For several hours Vasco and the other males had tried to reach it by climbing on top of each other's backs, but to no avail.

Later, at the other end of the hold, Vasco noticed a large rectangular opening a few centimeters from the ground. But he realized that it didn't offer any hope either, for in the center of the opening was a fan that whirled at full speed. Any rat who ventured there would end up sliced to bits.

It had been a nightmare ever since. The old rags and pieces of abandoned rubber they found in the hold had all been nibbled. There was no food. And there was no way out.

Vasco let himself down heavily on his front paws. He felt responsible for what was happening. His ears continually pricked up as he followed each move of his companions: some were agitated, some slept with one eye open. Signs of tension were becoming more obvious. Vasco didn't know how much longer his companions could endure their predicament before violence erupted.

Even Regus seemed to lose courage. He spent his time curled up next to the females, waiting for some miracle. Vasco no longer dared to approach him.

The only one who still seemed to have the will to overcome exhaustion and hunger was Lek. He tried relentlessly to gnaw at the door and walls. He ran from corner to corner, exhorting his companions to help him, but in vain. Vasco let him be: a busy rat did not have time to think about hunger.

In one of the corners, the females had built something resembling a nest. They huddled together under Joun's watch. A smell of curdled milk emanated from their bodies. One of the females had just given birth to a litter of five. Vasco inhaled this enticing smell and was envious of the young ones—at least they had something to eat. But for how long? *What's the use of giving birth to babies if they're doomed at the bottom of a boat?* he thought sadly.

Shaking himself, Vasco left his lookout point and went again to inspect the fan. His ears pricked as he listened to the purring noise of the motor.

Then, in the dark, he felt Nil's presence. The young female touched him slightly with her whiskers and rubbed her flanks against his. Vasco could feel the protruding bones of her ribs. Nil, who had been so well fed in Akar's tribe, was now becoming skinnier than a wild rat.

"I'm hungry," Nil whispered.

Vasco lowered his snout, embarrassed.

"Regus says that we're going to die," Nil went on. "But you'll save us, won't you?"

Her voice was imploring. Vasco knew that ever since he had saved her life on the harbor, the young female trusted him. But what could he do for her now?

High-pitched cries suddenly gave him a start. A fight had erupted in the females' corner. Vasco rushed over, guided by the groans of the males, the angry hisses of the females, and the grating of claws on the metal floor. He found two furious males standing on their hind legs. They were trying to grab the females' throats. Behind them, the newborns crawled blindly, defenseless and vulnerable. Before Vasco had time to act, a third male managed to cross the bulwark of females. Quickly, Vasco sprang forward and fell on the back of the attacker, forcing him to let go of the young rat he had grabbed in his mouth. Vasco bit him until he bled. The other cried out in pain.

Vasco called for help. "Regus!"

The wounded rat turned and threw himself at Vasco with rage. Vasco moved back, just avoiding being bitten. He could hear the frightened and vindictive cries of the female who was gathering her little ones under her belly to protect them. Behind him, Lek came to the rescue but there was no response from Regus.

The male who had nearly succeeded in devouring the baby rat circled Vasco in defiance, as if he wanted to forget his hunger by fighting. Farther away, Lek was coping with the other hungry males. The situation that Vasco feared most was unfolding: madness was taking over.

"Regus!" he called again.

A smell of blood and fear invaded his nostrils. He had no choice. When his adversary leaped toward him again, Vasco gave a harsh cry and reared as high as he could. His mouth wide open, his claws bared, he took the first blow, then violently snapped his teeth on the snout of the male, who collapsed and squeaked before running off. The other males spat and bristled their fur but no longer tried to come near the baby rats. Joun managed to shelter them behind a pile of rusty chains. Gradually, the cries died down. The males scattered and a heavy silence fell over the tribe.

Short of breath, Vasco and Lek relaxed their muscles, still on their guard.

"We avoided the worst," Lek whispered, shuddering. "I'll stay near the females and watch over the little ones."

As Lek moved away, Vasco turned when he picked up Regus' scent behind him. The beige rat was standing alone at some distance.

"I called you," Vasco said.

"You managed without me," Regus pointed out.

Vasco approached his friend. "I needed your help," he murmured.

"I should not have followed you," Regus said.

115

"Coming aboard this freighter was a mistake." Without saying anything more, he moved away and disappeared in the darkness of the hold.

Vasco's spirit was broken. He dragged himself next to the fan and lay down on the cold floor. The motor was still purring. Sometimes it seemed to slow down, then in a kind of hiccup speeded on again. Vasco felt a burning sensation in his belly. A little blood trickled out, reddening his fur. He licked his wound. Under his paws, the freighter kept on vibrating and pitching, taking the tribe to an unknown destination.

What if Regus is right? Vasco wondered. *What if this freighter ends up being our coffin?*

2

On the Other Side of the Fan

Whenever he had time to think, Vasco thought about all
he had left behind: the city, the harbor, and the warehouse where he was born. But he also remembered the
trucks that patrolled the streets and hounded the rats
well into the sewers. What the humans had planned was
merciless: none of the city rats, even those hiding deep
underground, would elude them. So there had been little
choice but to escape by sea. It was imperative that they
find a new shelter.

The air exhausted by the blades of the fan was

charged with scents of salt mingled with warm steam. Vasco knew that behind this wall were places where they would find food. But was there a way to stop the fan?

Nil came out of the dark. She loitered nervously around Vasco as she swished her tail.

"I'm afraid!" she said. "The males are losing their minds."

Vasco tried to calm her. Brushing against her, he could feel her heart beating in the vast silence that surrounded them.

"One of the newborns is wounded," Nil went on. "It's a female. She probably won't survive."

Vasco grew uneasy. The silence was strange. And all at once, he understood. He turned toward the fan. That was it—the motor was not purring. The fan had completely stopped.

In two strides Vasco slipped between the blades and emerged on the other side. He squeaked to call Nil, but sensed her hesitation as she neared the hole in the wall. So he squeaked some more to alert his other companions. Finally Nil took the plunge. He could see her snout between the blades. Pushing herself with her hind legs, she wiggled through and fell by his side. The other members of the tribe were growing restless. In the dark, they tried to locate the spot from which Vasco was calling.

"This way, Regus!" Vasco cried when he picked up Regus' scent.

But just as Regus was about to slip through, the fan began to whirl again. Regus stopped just in time. Nil sent a desperate squeak. Over the noise of the motor, the other rats answered with similar cries that echoed on their side of the metal partition.

Vasco was disconcerted. "It's going to stop again," he told them, trying to be hopeful. "We have to wait."

He stayed huddled next to Nil, and together they observed the spinning blades of the fan, attentive to the slightest hiccup of the motor. On the other side of this frightening machine was a tribe of prisoners. Vasco still trembled at the idea that he was free. He waited, his heart pounding, and paid no attention to the spot where he had just landed. He simply focused on the moving blades of the fan and was overcome with a feeling of helplessness. What if luck did not repeat itself?

After a while, Nil moved away from him. Her snout to the ground, she wandered about. When she came back, she jostled Vasco.

"There's an exit over there," she said. "Let's go find food." Food! Vasco suppressed a shudder.

"No," he said. "I have to save everyone! Let's wait some more."

Nil squeaked and pulled him by the ear. On the other side, Vasco had been able to control his hunger. But now that he was free, the bitter taste in his mouth returned, as did the knot in his empty stomach. He looked at the fan and got up. He hesitated. Nil was pressing him, trying to drag him along to the exit. Inviting odors floated in the air. Vasco's nostrils moved rapidly, in rhythm with his heartbeats. Finally he surrendered.

"Let's go!" he said, taking off.

The unfamiliar world of the freighter lay before them, full of promise. Luck had given them a chance to escape their prison and at last they were going to eat.

First they crossed an empty hold similar to the one where they had been trapped. But this space opened onto a narrow gangway along which ran very hot pipes. Nil and Vasco followed the pipes until they reached a metal staircase. Dizzy with hope, both rats darted toward the top of the steps.

Their paws scratched the metal, their panting breath mingled with the muffled purr coming from the machinery. On the landing, Vasco slowed down and came to a stop. He listened and inhaled the surrounding air, which was saturated with humidity. No scents of food were discernible. Only warm steam and the greasy smell of motor oil came from the machines. No human was in sight.

Reassured, Vasco started off again, with an impatient Nil running feverishly by his side. They entered a large room where dozens of pipes converged and where huge square conduits rose to the ceiling. Steps as steep as a firehouse ladder also led to the deck above. Vasco hesitated.

Which way to go? It was Nil who decided to take the steps. They made their way upward in an attempt to leave the deserted belly of the freighter and find traces of life above. Vasco followed Nil as he tried to push thoughts of the tribe out of his mind. He convinced himself that Lek would be able to maintain peace among them. So in spite of his qualms, he had no other desire than to eat.

Suddenly Nil stopped. She went up on her hind legs and sniffed the air with care. So did Vasco. At the top of the steps, a smell lingered—a smell of something fermented.

"Bread," Nil whispered, coming down on all fours.

Vasco's stomach contracted even more. With swift strides, both rats found themselves facing an air vent at the bottom of a partition. That was where the smell was coming from. They started gnawing frantically at the plastic grid. After some furious efforts, they managed to widen the hole. Nil was the first one through. But Vasco was right on her heels, no longer able to control the flood of saliva that was frothing at his mouth. The two rats rushed ahead as fast as they could along the long straight duct that led to the kitchens.

3

Olmo

Vasco ran. He ceased to think anymore. He was just a famished animal, and being so close to food drove him wild. His legs beat against the duct, his nostrils flared to capture the delicious odor, and his whole body steeped itself in the smell. He was just a mouth, a wide-open mouth ready to bite, tear, and swallow at all costs.

At the end of the duct was another plastic grid. But this one had already been gnawed at. Teeth marks were visible, accompanied by an alien smell. Vasco sensed the presence of another rat. He stopped, suspicious. Nil pushed him on, out of breath and trembling with excitement at the smell of bread.

Vasco stepped cautiously through the grid and put his paws on a tiled floor covered in sawdust. A strong light shone from the ceiling. He was about to enter farther into the kitchen when a man's shouts made him freeze. Vasco had just seen a frightened rat dash by, then a broomstick that was chasing the rat. He stepped back, bumping against Nil. Things were falling down in the kitchen and the man's shouts grew louder. The chased rat ran in zigzags, squeaking under the blows.

"We've got to help him," Vasco murmured.

Nil shook her head. "It's too risky!"

Vasco turned toward her. Had she forgotten what it was like to be threatened by a human? Had she forgotten the bang of the shovel against the paving stones, not to mention the smell of hot metal when she had nearly been killed on the harbor? Had she forgotten that she had squeaked just like this unknown rat? Without waiting for her, Vasco took off, his paws skidding on the sawdust. He was blinded by the strong light but rushed ahead, guided by the noises. Suddenly he saw the rat, coming full speed right in front of him.

Vasco jumped aside and received a blow from the broom that sent him rolling under a table. The other rat rushed toward the duct but the man was already on top of him. His boot-covered foot just barely missed the rat's head. Vasco instantly popped out of hiding to attract the man's attention. At the same time, Nil appeared—she had gotten the message. In the midst of the turmoil, the three rats fled in different directions. This completely disoriented the man, who was so surprised by the number of rats that he held the broom in midair. That was all it took. With lightning speed, Nil and Vasco scurried back to the shelter of the duct. The alien rat was already there, cowering in the dark, exhausted and breathless with fright. But he was not alone. Behind him were two other black rats.

Vasco's stomach knotted up when he noticed that the larger of the two was looking at him with sharp, intense eyes. The rat was enormous. Vasco knew he would never have the strength to fight him.

"You're on my territory," the huge rat challenged. "Had you not helped one of mine, I would kill you."

Nil came forward courageously. "Vasco is our chief!" she said. "All we want is to eat."

The huge rat spat and Vasco saw the fur on his back bristle. "I am Olmo, the chief of the rats on this ship," he said. "Whatever is on board is ours."

Vasco looked at the rat he had just saved. It was a young one. His dark fur was speckled with breadcrumbs and sawdust. This rat might make a good bargaining tool.

"We're not trying to conquer your territory," Vasco said, turning to Olmo. "We'll stay on board the ship just as long as the voyage lasts. Then we'll disappear."

Olmo sniffed the air as if trying to ascertain Vasco and Nil's credibility. Watching him more closely, Vasco realized that the chief was rather old. His tribe was probably unused to interlopers, having cut itself off from the rest of the world a long time ago. Vasco decided not to incite a useless conflict.

"Leave us in peace until the journey ends," Vasco said, feeling emboldened. "We'll be discreet. We do not like to fight."

To make himself more convincing, Vasco folded his front legs and lowered his snout to the ground. It was a risky move, but Vasco had the feeling that the old chief was intelligent. He would realize that Vasco was willing to submit to the chief's law.

"Never come into the kitchens," Olmo said finally. "Find your food elsewhere, and don't stir up our anger. In exchange, we'll leave you be."

Olmo then walked farther into the duct and signaled the others to follow him. Within seconds, they vanished. Nil sighed in relief. Vasco knew she would not have had the strength to take on these black rats, any more than he would have. She turned toward the opening of the duct, and with her he breathed in the smell of bread and flour.

Her stomach must be torturing her the way his was. Still, Vasco knew he had to keep his pledge.

"No," Vasco said. "We have an agreement with Olmo."

Nil regretfully followed his lead and they returned to the duct through which they had entered. Soon the duct divided itself into many elbows and junctions. Vasco and Nil groped their way, in fear of meeting other rats. Seized by panic, they started to run until a glimmer of light showed them the way out. They found themselves in an unknown gangway. There were no smells of food to excite their nostrils, which meant they had probably descended to the bottom of the ship.

Running at full speed, they darted across deserted rooms, along dark gangways, and through bulkheads where night-lights were blinking. The freighter was immense, hostile, and cold. Vasco could imagine it plowing the waves, tiny in the immensity of the sea. He felt far tinier himself. He thought about Nil's words: *Vasco is our chief*. As an orphan of the harbor, and as a young, inexperienced rat, he felt uncomfortable being referred to as a chief. In fact, if he were really the tribe's chief, he would have remained with his own and not have gone running off to satisfy his selfish appetite.

Vasco slowed down. He heard the grating of chains somewhere above his head. The noise of the machines was deafening. He and Nil were now in a large, dimly lit room. An entanglement of metal gangways rose to the ceiling. The dominant scents they picked up were those of human sweat and of chemicals used for the upkeep of the engines.

Now an echo of voices reached their ears. It was coming closer. The gangways shook with footsteps. A crude light suddenly flooded the large room. Vasco and Nil rushed to a corner. A few meters above them, men in blue overalls set themselves in front of a console. They could hear the noise of tools and the sound of laughter. The two rats exchanged a knowing look: alone in such unfamiliar surroundings, they didn't stand a chance. Vasco signaled to Nil that they had to go back to the others in the hold.

If I'm their chief, Vasco thought, *I have to find a way to stop the fan.*

4

Supervised Freedom

Vasco noticed a dark passageway underneath the engine room. He slipped inside, followed by Nil. No human could stand up here. The spot was located between two layers of planks and was filled with pipes and plenty of nooks. It was warm—the perfect hiding place. Vasco explored the premises and discovered several ways out.

Their snouts in the air, Nil and Vasco left the area and tried to orient themselves. They went from one hold to the other, using stairs to go down to the very bottom of the freighter. Finally they found the room where the square pipes joined together, and they recognized their route. Going still farther down, they reached the hold with the whirling fan.

Vasco placed himself in front of the spinning blades and squealed. Right away, another squeal answered his. It was Lek. He seemed jumpy. In spite of the noise of the fan, Vasco made out other squeaks that clued him in to the high tension among the prisoners. Lek relayed that some males had tried to eat the newborn rats again. This time Regus had intervened. That was a good sign. Regus was coming back to his old combative and kindly self.

"But Hog has disappeared!" Lek added.

Vasco shuddered at the news. He knew Hog was strongheaded and had probably taken advantage of an interruption in the fan to pass through to the other side. If he went hunting on Olmo's territory, he would unknowingly break the agreement.

"You have to take us out of here!" Lek begged.

Vasco began to turn in circles near the fan, unsure of what to do. There was no way to simply stop this machine.

Nil had come back and was pulling a heavy, thick piece of wood between her teeth. Silently and painstakingly, she dragged it over to the fan. Vasco looked at her, puzzled. Finally he understood her purpose and leaped to the side of the young female. The piece of wood was difficult to manipulate, but seated on their tails, the two rats planted their claws in the grooves and managed to place it vertically in front of the fan. The rats on the other side continued their agitated squeaks.

The wood was positioned. Vasco stepped back, as did Nil. Then Vasco listened to the threatening purr of the motor. If he failed, he would die, crushed by this hellish machine. But if he succeeded . . .

In a flash he ran toward the piece of wood, and in one leap pushed it toward the hole with a swift kick of his foot. He angled his flexible body sideways in midair and landed on the ground. There was a sudden snap, followed by a few mechanical jolts, and then . . . everything stopped. The piece of wood was stuck between the blades of the fan. At last, the machine was idle.

After a few seconds of surprise, the prisoners began to squeak. They congregated near the fan, unsure of their safety. Regus was the first to go through the blades. Vasco sighed in relief when he saw the nose of the beige rat. As soon as he was free, Regus rushed to Nil and rubbed himself against her with happiness. Vasco stayed back, his heart curiously heavy. Had the ordeal of confinement and hunger destroyed the trust that united him and Regus?

One by one the rats of the tribe extricated themselves from their prison. Lek gave priority to the females, who had difficulty going through the blades with their little ones clutched between their teeth. Once they were all safely assembled around Vasco, Lek signaled to the males. At each passage, the blades shook and threatened to resume their deadly spinning. But the piece of wood stood firm. Lek was the last one to clear the obstacle. Now the whole tribe was free—a horde of famished rats let loose at the bottom of the ship.

Vasco took a deep breath and stood up among them. He knew he had to quiet the fervor that was taking hold of them.

"We are not the only ones on board the ship," he announced.

He recounted his meeting with Olmo and the agreement the two had reached. When he finished, Regus stepped forward, tense and suspicious.

"Apart from the kitchens, where can we find food?" he asked.

The others showed signs of agitation again.

"I don't know," Vasco confessed. "But Olmo's tribe is surely larger than ours. We must avoid a battle."

"He's right!" Lek exclaimed. "Too many of us would die."

Vasco explained that he had discovered a place below the engines, a nook where they would all be safe. Once settled there, the strongest among them would go look for food.

"What about Hog?" Lek asked.

"We'll search for him at the same time."

"But if he comes back here, how is he going to find us?"

Vasco appointed two young males to stand guard near the fan in case Hog returned.

Several males protested this decision and spat to show their resentment. If Vasco hadn't been there to stop them, they would have rushed to the kitchens. Time was of the essence. Vasco looked at Regus, who stood apart from the others as if he wanted to regain his independence. But Vasco knew that as long as they were on this freighter, in the middle of the ocean, the only way to survive was to stay united.

"Follow me and I promise that we'll find something to eat!" he declared.

He looked at Regus. Pushed by Nil, the beige rat rejoined the group.

"Let's go!" Vasco said as he ran to the back of the hold.

Along the gangways and hot-water pipes, in the warm and humid atmosphere of the fume collector, up the steep ladders and narrow ducts that he had memorized, Vasco guided his group. It made him remember his trip across the city where trucks were looking for rats. It made him remember the fright that had knotted his belly. Would he have to spend his whole life fleeing and hiding? The memory of Akar flooded back with force. Akar . . . the very sound of that name made Vasco tremble. Panting, he stopped. The rats gathered around him pricked their ears. Vasco managed to slow his heart. Akar was no longer here. He had remained ashore and was probably dead now, killed by humans.

"I can smell the odor of men," Lek said to Vasco.

They were just at the entrance of the engine room. A beam of light shone on the other side of the bulkhead.

"One by one, behind me!" Vasco ordered.

Carefully he entered the large room and slid into the nook that led to the hiding place.

5

Ruckus in the Kitchen

As soon as the tribe had settled in, Vasco gathered a dozen of the males. The rats Vasco had fought in the hold were among them. A wound could be seen on one of their heads. But this was not the time to settle old scores. The expedition was dangerous, and coming back empty-handed was out of the question. At length, Vasco insisted on the precautions to be taken. Olmo must not see them. It was in the best interest of the hunters to make themselves as unobtrusive as ghosts.

"What about Hog?" Tiel and Coben reminded him, joining the group.

The brother and sister were worried and edgy, and they arrogantly curved their backs to show that they were ready to go hunting with the adults. Vasco hissed. Tiel and Coben would not be allowed to leave the nest.

"I'll keep an eye on them," Lek said as he pushed them back toward the females.

At that moment, Regus emerged from the shadows. "I'll come with you," he said as he placed himself next to Vasco.

The signal was given and the rats left their hiding place. They ran noiselessly to the decks above, hunger and fear knotting their bellies.

Regus moved swiftly, his nostrils flared. His presence reassured Vasco, who remembered how nimbly his companion had taken him through the hostile streets back in town. The solitary Regus had survived attacks from stray cats, men, and belligerent rat tribes for so long that the dangers of the freighter did not frighten him.

As they went up a duct and along a water pipe, Vasco caught a whiff of an appetizing smell. The others behind him trembled. It was the smell of spoiled meat and it came from a deck above. They stopped when they reached the end of the duct. A dim light flooded the spot. They heard the clatter of dishes and sounds of human voices singing along with a radio. Vasco moved forward and put his snout out. His heart thumped in his chest. A man's legs were very close to him. He retreated near the others.

This isn't the kitchen, Vasco thought. *We're in the scullery.*

Breathing in the smells, he detected those of cleaning products but also of vegetable peels. There had to be orange rinds and apple skins piled up in the open garbage bag. A flood of saliva filled his mouth.

"Wait a little longer," he said to his companions, who were prancing with impatience.

They remained motionless a long while, observing the man's legs. At last, the man left his post and the way was clear. Vasco and Regus went first. They found themselves under a sink. Poking their heads out, they discovered a room equipped with huge pieces of steel equipment. At the other end, they spotted several men bustling around carts that were piled high with trays. As for the garbage bag, it stood in the middle of the room, a magnet of temptation, and fully exposed.

"Now!" Regus said.

Not waiting for Vasco's authorization, Regus darted across the room, his paws scratching the tiled floor. Blood rushed to Vasco's temples. He looked at the men, one of whom moved away from the group. Regus sensed the danger and managed to slip behind the garbage bag. The man emptied one of the trays into it and returned to his station, whistling. Vasco sighed in relief. He saw that Regus had begun to gnaw at the bottom of the garbage bag. A look right, a look left, and Vasco silently joined his companion.

In no time, the two rats had ripped open the bag. Vegetable peels, empty yogurt containers, rice grains, chicken bones, and stale bread crusts spilled out. Temptation was so strong that Vasco and Regus started to nibble at everything they could find.

Under the sink, the other males could no longer wait. Forgetting all wisdom, they swarmed the garbage bag. Vasco looked up when he heard their disorderly race. The men were going to see them for sure! He stood on his hind legs and dropped his piece of meat. Now the pack of rats was huddled around the trash spread on the ground.

Vasco plucked enough courage to look toward the men near the carts. At that moment, one of them turned back. He had heard something over the noise of the radio and approached the garbage bag.

Vasco sent out a warning squeak. Regus registered the message right away. He grabbed a piece of meat between his teeth and fled toward the sink. The man started to shout. He ran behind Regus. Losing no time, Vasco signaled to the others. Each one grabbed as big a piece of food as possible. For his part, Vasco carried a large orange peel. In a split second, he noticed another way out: the door of the scullery was open!

He leaped to the door with the other males. Human

clamors echoed in the large room. The men were now rushing in all directions, heels ready to crush the intruders. But the rats were quick and took advantage of the surprise they created. They all reached the opening in good time. The men started to run behind them.

Vasco and the others hustled at full speed into a large room. They noticed tables attached to the ground and saw sailors drinking and smoking on benches. They had entered the mess hall! Panicked, the rats dispersed under the tables. Shouts burst out. Feet were raised and came crushing down close to them. Vasco veered every which way to avoid the kicking feet and projectiles. He looked anxiously for his companions, who were dispersed around the room. Where to flee? A noise made him jump: a fork had bounced not far from his snout. Then knives, spoons, and lighters followed. Vasco jumped from side to side, ran straight ahead, then darted back. He didn't see any way out! The men regrouped and tried to circle the rats. The end was near; the trap was closing in on them.

6

A Smell of Blood

Strident and steady beeps went off. The sound was coming from gadgets attached to the sailors' belts, bringing the men to a halt. Somewhere something was happening that required their immediate presence. They stopped chasing the rats and left the dining hall on the double to man their posts. In the turmoil that followed, Vasco and his companions rushed back to the scullery, toward the duct they had used on their way in.

Once in the shelter, they caught their breath. Regus had a piece of meat between his teeth. Vasco approached him.

"That place is very dangerous!" he whispered. "We almost got killed."

Regus didn't respond. He breathed in the sour smell emanating from the group of survivors.

"Dangerous . . . but well supplied," he said after a while, clearly satisfied.

It was true. Vasco couldn't help noticing that in spite of everything, the loot was substantial. Every rat had managed to snare a piece of meat, bread, or fruit.

"The others are waiting for us," Vasco said. "Let's head off."

With renewed confidence, Vasco and the others went down the duct. The risk had been high but worthwhile: for the first time in several days, their bellies were full. Vasco was also filled with contentment as he imagined the welcome they would receive from the famished females and their hungry babies. The unity of the tribe was certain for now. As long as they could find food, Vasco would be able to rely on everyone's cooperation. A feeling of elation took hold of him. Maybe the remainder of the trip would prove eventless.

But as they neared the end of the duct, the rats stopped abruptly. Their nostrils were assailed by a strong smell of fresh blood. They sniffed in the dark. Suspicion made them freeze. Beyond the smell of blood, Vasco recognized Olmo's scent.

"The black rats," he whispered. "They were here just a moment ago."

Vasco advanced slowly, his ears pricked. After the din in the dining hall, the silence on the landing of the metal staircase was surprising. A strange atmosphere had invaded the bottom of the freighter. Vasco shuddered. He moved farther ahead, with Regus close on his heels.

The smell of blood intensified on the first step of the stairs. Vasco put down the orange peel he was carrying between his teeth. On the second step, he finally discovered where the smell of blood was coming from. The body of young Hog lay torn to pieces.

Vasco heaved and turned away. Hog had obviously met up with Olmo. The dominant rat of the freighter had warned that he would be merciless! Unknowingly, Hog had broken the agreement: he had ventured somewhere he was not supposed to and paid for it with his life. A cold rage invaded Vasco. He remembered the terrible morning on the harbor when he discovered that his tribe was missing. He remembered, too, the intense feeling at finding Hog, Tiel, and Coben. For the first time in his life, Vasco had felt the urgency to protect someone other than himself. Hog had even survived the madness of men . . . only to succumb to Olmo's savage attack.

Regus pressed Vasco. "The hiding place!" he said.

Vasco's thoughts were muddled. If the agreement was

broken, Olmo might attack the others to be rid of the intruders altogether. Regus was right: they needed to return to the nest in a hurry! But Vasco remained stunned in front of Hog's corpse. Then, in a daze, he went up the two steps, grabbed the orange peel and placed it near the young rat's bleeding nose. The others were impatient: why lose time over a dead rat?

"Let it be," Regus said. He seemed to understand that Vasco needed to pay tribute to Hog, but he leaped over the corpse, leading the others away.

Vasco stayed in front of Hog's shredded body. An immeasurable sadness welled up in him, commanding silence, as if with Hog's death a part of himself had died as well. Now only Tiel, Coben, and he were the remnants of their native tribe. Three rats lost out at sea.

Eventually Vasco shook off his musings and bounded over all the steps of the metal staircase, landing on all fours.

7

Breach of Agreement

Cries greeted the males as they entered the hiding place. They burst in, claws out, ready to fight. But the deafening noise was merely the group of famished young rats and females who had been waiting so long that they snatched at the food. Vasco was too relieved to mind being jostled by them. Olmo was not there. Soon the cries were replaced by the grating of teeth and groans of satisfaction. At last the tribe was eating!

As stomachs were being filled, Vasco took a survey of the various exits in the nook. He sniffed at each with care, making sure that Olmo had not followed their scent marks. He hadn't. The black rats had obviously been satisfied with their encounter with Hog.

Vasco joined the others, casting a glance at Tiel and Coben. The brother and sister were sharing a discolored banana peel. Their whiskers glistened in the dark. In spite of the ordeal of the last few days, they had grown a lot. Their muscles too were bulkier. They were adults now. Vasco had fulfilled his responsibilities toward them. As for Hog, Vasco hadn't been around to prevent him from running away, something he knew would be a lifelong regret.

Joun and Lek approached him and rubbed themselves against him in thanks. He had saved the tribe. The female who was nursing her young would be able to continue. Even her wounded infant had not died. But this offered little comfort to Vasco, who remained somber and preoccupied. He looked for Regus.

Scurrying from one corner to the other, he finally found his friend in the company of Nil. The young female was coiled around Regus' flank, eating pieces of meat she tore from a bone. Vasco stopped a few steps away from them and hesitated. He did not want to disturb their intimacy. The sadness he had experienced in front of Hog's lifeless body was now accompanied by a strange feeling of abandonment. He looked at Nil: he, too, longed to feel her warmth against his side. But Regus was in the way, and considering the doubts that the beige rat had expressed about him, Vasco did not dare try to dislodge him. It would be a useless fight. For the good of the tribe, Vasco knew he must maintain the friendship, however tenuous, that linked him to Regus.

Suddenly the beige rat raised his head and approached Vasco. His cheerfulness and carefree attitude of the past had returned. The expedition had restored his courage.

"We won't be able to go back to the scullery," Vasco said, trying to hide his distress. "The men will be on their guard."

"I'll find other places," Regus answered, full of confidence.

Vasco swung his tail from left to right and rubbed his snout with his paws. He was worried. Now that the agreement was breached, Olmo was a potential enemy. He had to warn the others. Overcoming his fear, he spoke to the tribe. The rats stopped feasting in an instant and pricked their ears to listen to him. Vasco told them about the discovery at the top of the stairs: how Hog's body had been torn to pieces. Right away, Tiel and Coben rushed over to him. They huddled against one another, their fur standing on end. In their eyes, Vasco read fear and hatred. Other males displayed anger. A murmur loaded with violence spread among the tribe: if the agreement was breached, nothing prevented them from hunting on Olmo's territory. Most of the males seemed ready to fight, while the distressed females convened.

Vasco caught Lek's gaze. Lek was waiting for orders. But Vasco felt discouraged.

"The voyage may be over soon!" he declared. "We have to keep our promise and avoid any bloodshed!"

Next to Vasco, Regus scratched the ground with his claws. Several females started to squeak, and several males grumbled that they refused to have their behavior dictated by Olmo.

"We managed to get rid of Akar," one of them said. "We can't let another tyrant take his place!"

Immediately, silence swept over the rats. Akar's name brought back old fears. Lek, who had been abused under Akar, seemed to have been seized with terror, leaving him mute and powerless.

"If we're hungry, we'll eat!" another male spoke up.

The situation was spiraling out of Vasco's control. Most of the rats agreed: now that they had eaten, they were ready to wage war. This was precisely what Vasco wanted to avoid. Yet Hog's death filled him with hatred too.

In the turmoil, Regus started to speak. Vasco knew that most of the males would recognize his authority. Regus was not the tribe's leader but he had what it took.

"Let's put our faith in Vasco," Regus said. "He's brought us to this point, far from the men who wanted our death. I don't want to die aboard this freighter. I want to see what awaits us at the end of our journey."

Gradually calm was restored. The rats listened to Regus. Perhaps they imagined the outline of a port or an island not far off. A place that could be a refuge, a place where no Akar or Olmo would disturb the peace.

"We have to be patient," Vasco said. "We will find a new home."

With those words, he slipped off into the loneliness of the shadows. It had been a long time since he had really slept. Now that there was immediate danger, all he desired was rest. As he closed his eyes, he knew that Lek and Regus would watch over the tribe. He knew that he could rely on them.

8

On Regus' Trail

Vasco was awakened by Nil. The young female nibbled on his ear and sent out little squeaks. Regus had disappeared!

An adrenaline rush stiffened Vasco's muscles. Regus had told Nil that he was going on a reconnaissance tour, but that had been a while ago. Since then she had looked for him in the near surroundings without success. Someone would have to go farther into the freighter, and she was afraid. Vasco felt a lump form in his throat as he saw how worried Nil was. He shook himself. He wondered whether she would worry as much about him if the situation were reversed.

He got up. Around him, the tribe was asleep. The rolling of the ship was getting more noticeable. Somewhere on the decks above, an alarm sounded intermittently. There must be a big swell on the ocean.

Placing Nil and the rest of the tribe in Lek's care, Vasco headed for one of the exits of the hiding place. He preferred to move along the corridors of the freighter alone, so as not to expose the others to any potentially dangerous encounters.

Where should I look for Regus? he asked himself. *Did he wander off out of hunger or out of revenge?*

Vasco sniffed the ground and edges of partitions, trying to detect the very special scent of his friend. Gingerly he stuck his head in the engine room. Men in blue overalls were hammering on steel parts over the open gangways. The *clang-clang* echoed in the room and bounced off the walls. To gain time, Vasco decided to use the gangways to go directly up. It was risky, but since he was alone, he could take the chance.

He started his ascent, all the while trying to reassure himself that Regus was probably lost in the holds of the freighter as he searched for food. The beige rat wouldn't have breached the promise. He wouldn't have purposely gone to fight with Olmo's rats. He was much too sharp for that; besides, he had stated in front of the tribe that it was necessary to show moderation.

Vasco slipped along the dark corners as silently as possible. When he reached the first gangway, he sniffed Regus' scent. The beige rat had had the same idea and taken the same path! His body tucked in and his heart pounding, Vasco observed the men on the gangway above. There were only two of them. If he managed to reach the other side, he could escape them.

In front of him, the gangway crossed the fully lit room. It was a long and dangerous open stretch. But now that he was on Regus' track, he couldn't turn back. His whiskers were twitching. He looked up at the men, then down to the bottom of the room. If the situation turned dire, he could jump down and dash to the hiding place. Unless, of course, he got hurt when he fell.

Vasco moved on, now fully exposed. Above him, the tools kept on banging clearly and regularly. Vasco scurried along, not too fast, not too slow. He reached the middle of the gangway. Nothing happened. He kept on going. Suddenly a man swore. And a hammer landed on the gangway right behind Vasco. The whole metal bridge shook. Surprised, Vasco leaped forward and started to run. Surely the man had leaned over the bridge and seen him! But Vasco did not waste time to check. He ran at full speed and took refuge in the shadow of a large pipe.

Breathless, he dared to look toward the gangway. The man who had dropped his hammer was standing in the middle. He scrutinized the spot where Vasco was trying to blend in. Then with a shrug the man turned around and went the other way. Vasco felt immensely relieved. He had made it!

Now all he had to do was use the steps that ran along the pipe to reach the exit at the top of the room. Regus' scent was still here. The path was open in front of him.

Rising on his hind legs, Vasco grabbed the steps and climbed carefully. He could feel the cold of the metal pipe under the fine fur of his belly. From time to time, flakes of paint scratched his skin and dropped from the pipe in a faint clatter. Fortunately the men had resumed their work and were not paying attention to him.

At the top, the pipe formed an elbow and went horizontally through a partition. Vasco jumped onto the highest gangway. Regus' scent showed him the way out: four more steps up and a door opened onto a passageway.

There, Vasco lost Regus' scent. He looked around, hesitated, and stepped back. He found the scent again. Regus had probably rushed into the ventilation duct. Vasco followed the same route. When he entered the duct, he stopped. Somewhere an exhaust fan was sending out exhalations of food that tickled his nostrils. There was no doubt about it: Regus had wanted to eat!

After several turns, the duct plunged down to a brightly lit opening. Vasco let himself skid along this unexpected toboggan and gripped the flange that encircled the opening. The first thing he saw were chunks of frozen meat that were thawing. He had landed next to the freezers. The spot was deserted. In a glance, he noticed teeth marks on one of the chunks of meat. Regus had been here . . . and he had surely filled his stomach.

Vasco was about to leap forward when two dark shadows ran under the table. He spotted other rats coming out from another pipe. Without question, he knew this area was used as a pantry by Olmo's tribe.

9

The Sower of Dissent

Vasco tried to turn back but his paws slipped on the nearly vertical wall of the duct. He looked up. Retracing his steps was impossible. The only thing to do was to stay hidden on the flange and hope that Olmo's rats would not discover him.

From his vantage point, he surveyed the scene. The strongest males leaped onto the table. They sank their teeth into the brown meat and tore it to pieces. Small icy crystals caught in their whiskers, melting after a few moments. Leaning over the table, they threw the meat on the floor, where in an explosion of cries, females and young rats picked up the bits. Their mouths full, they dashed back toward the pipe from which they had come.

Vasco was flabbergasted. Seen from above, the comings and goings of the black rats resembled a tightly organized army of ants; pieces of meat fell from the table and were whisked off at incredible speed. Each time a rat left the room, another took its place. At this pace, an entire cut of meat was sure to disappear, bit by bit, into the pipe.

But now sharp squeaks reached Vasco's ears. The group of rats seemed agitated. The males on the table stood up, their snouts in the air. Vasco shook himself to warm up. His legs had become numb and were starting to hurt. So he moved ever so slightly, which caused one of the males to turn in his direction. He had just sniffed Vasco's presence.

But the black rat did not have time to investigate further. Shouts and noises that sounded like a stampede were getting closer. Then the pipe spat out a dozen scared young black rats into the room. The males jumped down from the table and regrouped on the ground.

Worried, Vasco twisted his neck, trying to make out the entrance of the pipe. But he was too far away and could only hear what was going on. It sounded like a fight was taking place in the pipe. Vasco wondered if Regus had been on Olmo's path.

The group of males then moved toward the pipe and the fighting intensified. Vasco heard cries, groans, and the grating of paws. The young rats in the room waited, on their guard.

After a long moment of confusion, silence returned. All the black rats left the room and disappeared into the pipe. Vasco was puzzled. What had just happened? His whiskers twitched; he could smell blood. But he couldn't say whether it was coming from the thawing meat or from something else.

As soon as he thought it was safe, he jumped from his hiding place onto the ground. He was no longer hungry. He simply wanted to know what drama had unfolded.

Everything seemed calm and deserted, so he noise-lessly slipped inside the pipe. The more he crept along, the stronger was the smell of blood. A few steps farther, he discovered two corpses, two black rats who had been bitten to death. Vasco sniffed them. Another scent hung around the two bodies—a scent that was not unknown to him. His throat tightened: Regus. Who else could have been here? But it was totally incomprehensible. What would have motivated his friend to sow dissent?

Vasco ran still farther into the pipe, until it branched out in several directions. In one, Vasco detected the scent of Olmo's black rats. So he opted for the other path and blindly tried to find his way back to the engine room. His heartbeat echoed in his head. He was breathing with difficulty, as if something heavy weighed on his chest. Regus couldn't possibly have betrayed him, and yet . . .

Suddenly he picked up the scent of the beige rat, who stood motionless at the end of the pipe. Vasco could see a shriveled shadow in front of Regus' paws. Dumbfounded, he realized that it was another corpse. His fur bristled. Regus sensed his presence and turned around.

"Vasco!" he shouted with relief.

"What have you done?" Vasco grumbled.

Regus looked at the corpse. "I just found him," he said. "He was already dead! And I found others! Something strange is going on!"

10

Tribe Against Tribe

Vasco and Regus stood face to face in silence. Their nostrils captured the dull smell emanating from the black rat's body. Vasco knew that Regus was telling the truth. But then who was the killer?

"It can only be a rat from our tribe," Regus murmured, feeling dejected.

"But who?" Vasco asked. "And why?"

Wasting no more time, they abandoned the pipe and started to run side by side to their hiding place.

When they reached the nook where the tribe was

gathered, they found Lek and Nil waiting for them. Nil rushed over to Regus.

"Did one of ours leave the nest?" Vasco asked.

"No, no one!" Lek assured him.

Vasco and Regus stepped over the sleeping rats but made such a din that they woke up the whole tribe. Vasco took a rapid head count: Tiel and Coben were here, surrounded by the females. None of the males was missing either.

As he was about to question each member of the tribe, he heard the noise of paws above his head. Some rats had entered the engine room, and their scent was now reaching this hiding place.

"Olmo!" Vasco shouted.

At that very instant, the chief of the black rats burst in. A good twenty rats streamed in behind him, in tight formation. Together Vasco and Regus faced Olmo. Their eyes met his shining gaze.

"I warned you!" Olmo roared. "You did not keep your word. Now you will die."

"Wait!" Vasco shouted. "None of us breached the agreement! Little Hog—"

"That one is dead!" Olmo cut him short. "He came into our nest and we chased him."

Vasco imagined the young rat's last moments and his throat tightened. In turn, Regus moved toward Olmo.

"I found some of *your* people dead," he said. "But we're not the ones who—"

Olmo rose on his hind legs. His erect posture made the old black rat look all the more imposing. Even Regus flinched. Talking was no longer possible. Olmo uttered a cry. The signal was given and his army fell upon Vasco's tribe.

Both camps confronted one another in a terrible uproar. With his teeth, Vasco managed to push back the two males who came after him. Around him, bodies intermingled, crashed, and rolled like barrels from one corner of the nest to the other. Cries and groans intensified. The females fled the attackers, squeaking with terror. Vasco was clawed. The temperature seemed to rise and his throat burned.

Then suddenly teeth sank into his flank. He cried in pain and picked himself up. But he stumbled, got up again, and opened his mouth as if to bite the darkness. His teeth didn't connect with anything. He jumped ahead and bumped against a motionless body. Then another. Wounded rats were crawling in all directions, looking for shelter. Vasco struggled on. He jumped over an enemy and grabbed his throat. The taste of blood filled his mouth. Shoved and thrashed, he no longer knew where the ground was. He felt as if he were floating through the air, bouncing from one body to another like a stone falling along a slope. He bumped against the walls and the pipes.

Fear buzzed in his ears. He did not feel pain anymore. He did not hear the cries. All he saw under the curled-up lips of his foes was the white gleam of their teeth. He moved like a robot, like a killing machine, scratching, biting, and jumping over all those in his way. The ocean, the freighter, the whole universe seemed to swirl around him like a madly spinning top. He swayed from right to left. Nothing had meaning anymore. There was only the darkness, the white of teeth, and the taste of blood. Nothing mattered but survival. Vasco was consumed by a savage force. He was drowning in his own violence. And he fought, eyes closed.

Suddenly the fighting stopped. Vasco was up on his hind legs, trembling in the middle of the nook. A few dead rats lay on the ground. Regus faced him, gasping for breath, blood drooling from his mouth. The squeaks of the wounded were fading away. Olmo had called back his tribe. The black rats were defeated.

Vasco felt he was emerging from a nightmare. Drops of blood ran down from his flank. The ground still moved under his paws but he was no longer flying, no longer a bouncing stone. Noises registered again in his ears, and like a painful wave, air inundated his compressed lungs. Vasco sent out a long cry and came down on all fours. He curled up, drained of all energy.

In the calm that followed the fight, squeaks could be heard. Vasco opened his eyes again and raised his head. Joun was standing in front of him. There was blood on her fur. Seeing her so out of breath, Vasco knew that she had struggled to the point of exhaustion.

160

"They'll be back," she said. "We have to hide somewhere else."

Vasco surveyed the battleground. He discovered three males of his tribe among the dead. One was the rat who had attacked the newborns when they had been locked in the hold. Vasco looked back at Joun.

"I don't know what happened," he said. "I don't know who killed Olmo's rats. I don't understand."

A limping Regus joined Vasco. "Where are the females?" he asked, worried. "And the young ones?"

Lek pointed to one of the exits of the nook. They had had time to find shelter in a corner of the engine room. None of them was hurt.

Something incomprehensible had happened, something that had destroyed the fragile balance that would have made cohabitation between the two tribes possible during the journey. Vasco felt extremely tired. A somber thought came to his mind: he wondered if he wouldn't have been better off dying on the harbor with his tribe instead of living such a violent and savage life. But did a leader have the right to let himself fall victim to despair?

Meanwhile, Regus headed toward the exit that Lek indicated. His legs could hardly support him but he turned and said, "I discovered a good hiding spot tonight. Follow me."

11

Swell on the Ocean

As Regus led his wounded fellow rats far from the engine room, an alarm went off. Its deafening sound echoed from deck to deck. Farther away, sailors were running loudly over gangways. Vasco now understood why he felt the ground move under his paws and why he had thought he was flying. Waves were making the ship pitch, waves big enough to shake this huge mass of a metal vessel. The storm had to be strong. From all sides, worrisome noises reached the ears of the rats: heavy blows struck the hull, and the chains made a deafening grinding sound. The strident howling of a siren confirmed the impression of danger.

Regus led the tribe through a suite of holds where crates were stowed, then through a network of pipes where he directed all of them to the deck above. At the rear, Vasco watched over the progress of the females, the young ones, and the wounded rats. From time to time, he caught sight of Regus. Regus, the independent spirit who refused to belong to any tribe, was now leading the rats. Nil trotted by his side, quick and nimble. So many events had happened since Vasco had saved her life on the port. So many things had changed since then.

Knocked around by the rolling of the ship, the tribe finally reached a large room that smelled of heat and detergent. No human was present: all the men had gone to their emergency stations. On one side of the wall, Vasco discovered a line of machines, each with a kind of glass porthole, and farther down were carts containing huge piles of gray laundry. Remains of perfumed vapors stagnated in the air.

"The laundry room," Regus announced. "Olmo will not come here."

Vasco joined the head of the tribe. There might be nothing to eat here, but it was warm, and the females would be able to tear pieces of fabric to build comfortable nests. The subdued glimmer of the night-lights gave the place a reassuring look. Regus had found a good spot.

While Joun distributed chores to the females, Vasco gathered the males around him. Again, hunger was palpable. They would have to forage for food. Vasco hoped that the storm would distract the sailors long enough to allow them to reach the kitchens. Now that Olmo had declared war, the whole ship was open to them.

The rolling of the ship worsened. Vasco called Lek and pointed to the carts that moved and rattled even though they were attached to the wall by a rope. The piles of laundry could easily topple onto the rats. Lek nodded in understanding. He would take care of everything.

As the rats were about to depart, another alarm sounded, this one different from the first. Then all at once, the lights went out. Vasco's heart pounded in his chest. He listened. Human shouts were heard on the decks above.

"Now is the time to go!" Regus suggested.

Vasco waited a little longer. He detected a noise, like a rumbling. Around him, the males were growing impatient. They were hungry.

"All right, let's go!" Vasco ordered.

The whole group headed toward an open bulkhead. Not far from them men were rushing down toward the hold. So the rats went in the opposite direction—up.

Vasco knew his way in this part of the ship. He had memorized the smells and the location of the main pipes and ducts. Finding his way back to the kitchen was not a problem. But while they climbed through the ducts, he stayed attentive to the rumbling noise. He wondered if it could be the roaring of water that he heard.

When they reached the end of the last duct, the rats poked their snouts out and observed their whereabouts. They found themselves under the kitchen sink. Unlike the first time, no radio was on. No man was whistling as he did the dishes. It was dark. The exhaust hoods above the stoves shook under the furious gusts of wind that swept the area. An icy and unsettling atmosphere hung over the place.

The rats came out of their hiding spot and scurried across the kitchen in single file. Regus and Vasco went straight to the trash and tore open the bag with their teeth. But this time nothing spilled out. Not even an empty can.

Disappointed, the group headed toward the carts. There again there was nothing to eat. Their snouts in the air, Regus and Vasco moved on. They passed the door and found themselves in the mess hall.

At last their expert nostrils detected the smell of food. Under the tables, they nibbled at leftovers of stale breadcrumbs, crushed peas, and greasy papers.

They carried this meager loot in their jaws and moved toward the duct to return to the laundry room.

When they reached the end of the duct, Vasco heard the rumble again. It was now stronger than before and with it came a blast of hot air. Vasco could feel the anxiety of his companions. He hurried down to the deck below, but as he came out of a gangway, he froze. The rumbling noise was the thunder of fire!

12

Shadows

The closer they came to the laundry room, the thicker was the smoke of the fire. It dried their throats and stung their eyes. The nauseating smell of burnt rubber permeated everything, causing panic among the rats. Their sense of smell was no longer of any help. They were disoriented and vulnerable.

As the group ran toward a bulkhead, the floor began to shake. Vasco clung to the base of the wall and so did all the others. A second later, pairs of feet clad in fireproof boots filed by, only a few centimeters from their snouts. A dozen men in tight formation grazed them. Vasco held his breath. None of the men noticed the small group of rats. As the noise of boots faded away, the rats sped off.

Now they approached the stairs. The steps seemed to have been swallowed by the smoke. Vasco stopped, hesitating. Any kind of danger could be hidden in this fog. . . .

But Regus rushed by.

"Wait!" Vasco shouted after him.

"No!" Regus answered.

He jumped into the smoke under Vasco's stupefied eyes. The other males were so panicked and unable to think clearly anymore that they followed the beige rat.

Alone on the landing, Vasco listened. The roar of the fire was now distinct. It had probably started in the hold or in the engine room. In any case, Regus and the others didn't stand a chance of reaching the laundry room. They would have to use another route to avoid danger.

Vasco walked back in the opposite direction. He passed through the bulkhead and the gangway again. He wanted to go to the deck above and come back down farther off. So he sped along, his throat burning as if he had swallowed flames.

The entire freighter now resonated with shouts. The alarm signals never stopped. Several times Vasco had to hide in nooks to avoid the men who rushed in all directions, pulling hoses behind them. Some compartments were closed off to stop the spread of the fire. Vasco roamed for a while in the complicated labyrinth of ductwork. At last, he found a way to the laundry room. He crossed dark corridors that led him through the mechanics' quarters and those of the officers. This part of the ship was deserted. The center of the fire was far away. Vasco breathed in clean air.

But as he reached the deck below, he realized that the smoke had already invaded everything. The heat was intense. The fire had spread over a great surface in all the holds. Now it was licking the partitions.

Vasco could see a dark shadow move on the ground. Then another. Considering the size of one of them, he supposed that it was Olmo. Noiselessly Vasco stepped aside. The two rats were not far from him now. He hid behind a metal pillar. The smoke irritated his throat. He wanted to spit. But he had to stay totally silent and motionless because the two shadows were coming in his direction.

As they neared, Vasco felt the heat of the fire. It was intense, and the smell was acutely acrid. His irritated eyes filled with tears. Yet the two rats did not seem afraid. They walked carefully, like hunters stalking prey.

Vasco waited a while longer, his back glued to the pillar. The rats were now extremely close.

Vasco refrained from shouting. A taste of death filled his mouth. It wasn't Olmo, the leader of the black rats. Before him Vasco saw a ghost, a horrible sight, a cadaver that had come back to life.

He knew the rat. It was Akar!

Vasco thought he was hallucinating. An orange light danced on the walls of the room. A muffled rumble, like a roll of thunder, erupted from the depths of the freighter. The two rats stopped a few steps away from him. In the light of the fire, Akar and his companion seemed immensely tall. Their shadows on the walls loomed threateningly. Vasco held his breath. The fear he felt when he had been hunting for Akar in the town sewers grabbed hold of him again.

Suddenly flames invaded the room. Vasco felt the heat in his nostrils. Akar and his accomplice gave a start. At the same moment, another rat emerged, running away from the flames. He came near the pillar where Vasco was hiding. It was Regus! His fur was singed and he was running for dear life. He didn't see Vasco, but he too noticed the presence of the two rats and slowed down. Vasco wanted to warn him but was too frightened to move. Paralyzed, he watched the scene like a spectator shielded behind a pane of glass.

Regus stepped forward with care. He was out of breath.

"Akar!" he shouted suddenly.

The two shadows came closer. Vasco could see them both. Akar was in front. Facing him, Regus went up on his hind legs. Akar's accomplice, one of his most faithful companions, remained behind, stunned.

Akar hesitated a second. The fire was gaining on Regus. A metal door was darkening and buckling. But Regus paid no attention. Here, in the middle of this ocean of fire, he had just found Akar, his blood brother, his worst enemy.

13

Water and Fire

That's the answer to the enigma! Vasco realized. *Akar is the one who killed Olmo's rats!* The possibility never would have occurred to him since he had believed that Akar was still on shore.

The fire was gaining ground. Far away, human voices could be heard, as well as the gush of water spurting out of fire hoses. If men didn't come soon, the room would turn into an oven. The ground warmed under Vasco's paws. Still he was unable to move.

A few steps away from him, Akar and Regus squared

off, united in mute hatred. They both stood on their hind legs, their fur on end. Suddenly Akar's companion recovered from his shock.

"You told us you killed Regus!" he shouted.

Akar turned around to face him. His lie was now discovered—Regus was here, very much alive and well. If news of this reached his tribe, his authority would be terminated.

All of a sudden there was a snapping noise. Vasco looked up. One of the pipes that ran under the ceiling had twisted and warped with the intensity of the heat and was falling. Regus jumped back, just in time. With a clang, the pipe crashed onto the ground, on the very spot where Regus had stood a second ago. Vasco couldn't even cry out. His whole body was frozen with fear. Above him, through the hole left when the pipe tore away, a shower of cold water poured into the room. As it made contact with the ground, the water turned into a cloud of steam.

Regus and Akar were now separated by the pipe. Men burst into the room through a door at the back. Regus jumped into a cavity, right in front of Vasco, while Akar threw himself on the other male. Both were lost in the smoke. Vasco didn't see anything more. Powerful jets of water tumbled on the ground with a hellish noise. Men wearing helmets and brandishing fire hoses moved forward, fighting the flames.

Vasco huddled against the pillar and was soon drenched to the bone. Around him, everything was swamped in water and smoke.

When the fog dissipated, he shook himself. The icy water had brought him back to his senses. He shivered and his teeth chattered, but he was able to control his movements. The group of humans finished putting the fire out. Drops of water fell from the ceiling, running along the walls and pipes. It looked as if a summer storm had broken out in the room and the sun would appear through the clouds any second. Vasco looked around him and spotted Regus, who was licking his paws. In a few leaps, Vasco joined him.

The two rats rubbed themselves against one another, happy to still be alive. The men were leaving—the fire had been put out. But one danger remained: where was Akar?

Regus and Vasco left their refuge without exchanging a word. They jumped over the fallen pipe. A little ways off, the dead body of Akar's companion lay on the ground, his throat slit open. As for Akar, he had disappeared in the smoke.

Vasco shuddered. Regus let out a hoarse noise. Now that they knew that their former leader was on board, they understood that the journey would not end without a bloody confrontation.

"Akar is looking for revenge," Regus murmured. "I humiliated him one time too many the day he wanted to kill Nil. He'll never leave me in peace."

Vasco thought with terror about the rats of Olmo's tribe that Akar had killed. Akar had played a strategic hand: Olmo believed it was Vasco who had attacked him, and so without knowing it he had become Akar's perfect ally. Now two tribes were trying to eliminate them.

"The laundry room!" Vasco whispered in anguish.

As fast as lightning, the two rats left the flooded room, running through the smoldering remnants of the fire. If flames reached their shelter, the whole tribe would die. Vasco wondered if he could survive the death of his own kind again. In front of him, Regus leaped ahead. Vasco guessed that his companion was particularly worried about Nil.

Finally the two rats reached the laundry room. The subtle smell of detergent had been replaced by the suffocating smell of burnt linen. Vasco stopped on the threshold. A desolate view met his eyes: the washing machines had had their windows broken and were all twisted, the carts were filled with incinerated sheets, and everywhere water was running down the blackened walls.

Regus started to run madly among the puddles and debris. He let out a piercing and desperate cry. Vasco also felt himself weakening. He took a few steps forward, sniffing the atmosphere. He knew only too well the scent of death, that dull smell that had emanated from Memona's body, from the rats killed by men, and, more recently, from the corpse of young Hog. But here in the laundry room, he did not detect that smell.

"I didn't find anything," Regus murmured. He seemed suddenly very old and very tired.

A noise attracted their attention. Turning around, they saw Lek and Nil hurrying their way.

They, at least, were alive.

14

Dark Thoughts

Nil rushed toward Regus while Vasco's eyes questioned Lek. Where were the others? The females, the young ones, Tiel and Coben? Lek got closer to Vasco, who could see that the other rat's coat was singed in many places. Lek rubbed his whiskers. After a bit, he recounted how the fire had entered the laundry room. Cornered by the flames, the rats had succeeded in gnawing part of the partition off.

Vasco contemplated the hole that Lek pointed out to him. On the other side, they had reached a kind of closet and ate away the rubber strip at the bottom of the door to get out.

Now Lek and Nil turned to Regus and Vasco with a spark of mischief in their eyes.

"We discovered a new hiding spot there," said Nil. "You'll see."

Lek and Nil bounded to the laundry room door. The two males followed.

A few seconds later, they emerged into a room with a strong odor of iodine. Vasco looked around him in amazement. Above his head, dozens of fish were hanging from hooks. And in one corner, the females, young ones, and adult males were busy tearing apart the flesh of a huge fish.

"This one fell off," Nil explained, her whiskers trembling at the prospect of the meal. She joined the feast.

Regus and Vasco approached rather timidly. Their stomachs were rumbling. When was the last time they had eaten something? And the last time they'd tasted fish? It was in the harbor . . . an eternity ago.

Vasco forgot the fire. He forgot Akar. He forgot his anxiety at the idea that he might find his tribe incinerated in the laundry room. He forgot Olmo and the men. Instead he pounced on the fish and pushed his snout deep into the grayish flesh. Nothing was as important as simply enjoying the moment.

For a while only groans of satisfaction and the clatter of teeth breaking fish bones could be heard. The rats of the tribe, all gathered in this dark place at the bottom of the smoke-filled freighter, were happy for the first time since boarding the ship. And in spite of the threatening uncertainty that lingered around them, they savored the salted flesh. They felt as if they were coming back to life.

Once his stomach was full, Regus joined Vasco and the two of them observed the others. They were the only ones aware of their dangerous predicament.

Then Lek joined them, followed by Joun and Nil. Their whiskers gleamed with fish oil, but their gazes remained worried. They sensed Vasco's uneasiness.

"Akar is not dead," Regus announced right away. "He's on the ship."

Lek tensed slightly. Nil opened her mouth but no sound came out.

"I don't know how, but he followed us," Vasco continued. "He's the one who killed Olmo's rats."

Joun began to tremble. She looked at the females and young ones still gathered around the fish. Now that the laundry room was destroyed, the tribe had no refuge. It was urgent to find a hiding place. Vasco shared Joun's weariness. To keep the tribe alive, they would have to settle in a permanent spot.

"What are we going to do?" Joun asked.

"I'll take care of it," Regus said. "It's for me to deal with Akar. Me alone."

Nil brushed against his side. She squeaked and swished her tail nervously. Lek dropped his head, and Vasco guessed that the fear Lek had felt when he lived in Akar's nest had overwhelmed him again. Joun sidled up to her mate. She clearly knew how he felt. Lek raised his head and looked at Regus with admiration and did not dare say anything.

"I'm going to ferret him out," Regus went on, his teeth set. "And this time, he won't survive."

Vasco shook his head. He didn't want Regus to confront Akar by himself. They had to stay together.

"If we find a hiding place," he whispered, "maybe Akar will not look for us."

Regus spat and arched his back. "Hide? Never! On the contrary, we must be ahead of him. We must surprise him!"

Regus was so confident that Vasco did not know what to say. While they discussed the best strategy, other males approached. Vasco could feel them full of vigor, ready to fight. Deep down, he knew that Regus was right, but the idea of another bloodbath disturbed him terribly.

Nil remained glued to her companion. "Don't go alone," she begged. "Listen to Vasco! Let's stay together!"

Then, shaking but determined, she added, "If we have to, we'll fight tribe against tribe."

All the rats approved of her determination. They didn't have a choice: either they got rid of Akar or Akar would get rid of them. And if not Akar, then Olmo.

"We have to act now," Regus pressed on.

Vasco resignedly asked Joun to guide the rest of the tribe to a new refuge on a higher deck—since the fire had destroyed the hold, the humans would no doubt invade this place to repair the damage. Vasco and his companions would meet up with the tribe once they had dealt with Akar.

• • •

Joun watched the group of hunters leave the fish reserve. She sighed when she saw Nil go off by Regus' side. The young female was brave but still ignorant of many things. Joun turned back. In a corner, Lek was seated on his hind legs, shaking and helpless. Under his singed coat, his skinny frame quivered with rage. He was unable to follow the other males. Joun licked his snout, then left him alone with his dark thoughts. For the time being, she knew, Lek was no longer free: his fear hampered him like a shackle at the neck of a slave.

15

Rendezvous on the Gangway

Regus, Nil, and Vasco led the file. Behind them, a good twenty rats readied to fight. Their bellies were full and their teeth were sharp. They climbed up the pipes toward the crew's quarters. Vasco had been this way before. He supposed that the sailors were far too busy dealing with the consequences of the fire to enjoy any rest time. This meant that the gangways and cabins would be deserted.

A long and straight corridor opened in front of them; it was empty. Night-lights cast bluish halos above the doors. Vasco pricked up his ears. Not a noise. In the silence, he realized that the swells still shook the ship. The storm wasn't over yet.

"The scent!" Nil shouted suddenly as she stopped.

Vasco looked at her and saw how vividly the odor brought back memories. Good or bad, they were a part of her life on the ground and had welled up from the depth of her recollections: the time in her life when she ate copiously by Akar's side. Fear altered her breathing slightly. More than ever, Vasco felt certain that he had to kill Akar, regardless of the price to be paid. As long as Akar lived, it would be impossible to secure the future of the new tribe.

Nil started to run down the corridor, followed by all the males. When they reached the end, they discovered another gangway that ran perpendicular to the first one. Vasco stopped. He took in small breaths, trying to fight a slight dizziness. Next to him, Nil and Regus squeaked with impatience. Their snouts in the air, they searched for Akar's scent.

Quite suddenly, some rats appeared out of a corridor, right in front of Vasco. The whole group gave a start.

"That's him!" Nil whispered.

"There are only four of them," Regus said.

Vasco did not wait and rushed forward. Behind him, the others pressed on, hearts beating wildly, teeth bared.

At the end of the corridor, Akar sent up a cry of alarm. Immediately he turned and fled with his companions. He understood that he did not stand a chance and preferred to retreat.

Seeing Akar disappear, Vasco increased his efforts. Now that he had made up his mind to act, he ran as fast as possible, side by side with Regus, focusing on one thing only: he had to kill this large rat, eliminate this tyrant. He could hear the others panting behind him, and his dizziness increased.

The four fugitives made a right turn and crossed an air vent. Over there! Vasco caught a glimpse of Akar as he went up a pipe. Vasco shot forward like a cannonball, with the others behind him. They climbed the pipe, bumping into each other in the dark.

In the distance, they could hear the paws of their enemies scratching the metal pipe. At last they reached the deck above and entered a deserted room. Akar was several meters ahead of them, running toward the exit.

At the other end of the room, a door opened onto a larger corridor, its floor covered by a carpet. The noises were muffled . . . but the scents weren't!

The rats advanced like a furious army through a corridor lit with warmer lights, and where cabins were spaced far apart. It had to be the officers' quarters. They reached a well-lit landing. The area was large. Vasco stopped running. There was something unusual about this spot.

"Up there!" Nil shouted.

Vasco looked above him and saw Akar's shadow pass in front of his eyes. He also realized that the bright light was coming from a glass dome that surmounted the area. For the first time since the beginning of the voyage, Vasco could see daylight. It took his breath away.

"Quick!" Regus shouted.

The beige rat took the lead and rushed up the steps. Vasco shook himself and joined the others on the ship's bridge. Through the glass, it was possible to see a mass of tormented clouds smothering the ocean. Akar and his companions had stopped at the end of the gangway.

Vasco was still dazzled by the light and did not immediately grasp the situation. He saw Akar walk back. Then Regus did the same. Standing up with difficulty, Vasco moved forward. He was light-headed. He felt as if he were entering into a fog. All this light around him . . . and those clouds rolling above. He could even hear the rain knocking against the glass.

"Vasco!" Nil whispered.

Suddenly the fog dissipated. Nil's voice jolted him and he registered an incredible sight: Akar was snout to snout with Olmo.

The leader of the black rats stood motionless and proud, and just as imposing as Akar. Did he understand who his real enemy was? Vasco watched him. Depending on Olmo's decision, the confrontation would turn to the advantage of one or the other party.

It's the final fight, Vasco thought with terror.

16

Lek's Decision

At the prow of the ship, Lek watched Joun gather the females around her and explain that she had just discovered a new hiding place for the tribe. It was a hold where metal barrels were stowed and held in place with dozens of tightly stretched straps woven together like a cobweb. The most nimble of the young rats were already playing among the intertwined straps, squeaking with happiness. Joun approached Lek and tried to comfort him. But his brain was tormented by contradictory feelings and he was no longer himself. His breath wheezed, and his body was racked by shudders.

"I should be with Vasco," he said.

Joun licked his flanks tenderly. "You should try to find food for the little ones instead," she suggested. "They're going to need it."

Lek glanced at the young ones. Seeing them scamper over the barrels almost fooled him into thinking that life was back to normal, free of worries. Even Tiel and Coben, who had been saddened by Hog's death, seemed to have regained their playful spirit. But Lek had only one thought: Akar was aboard the freighter. The idea was unbearable. Bitter saliva filled his mouth.

"You're right. I'm going off to hunt," he announced.

Out of the corner of his eye he saw Joun looking at him with apprehension as he set off. He knew he was weak and vulnerable—and he also knew that would never change as long as Akar was alive.

17

A Fight in the Thunderstorm

For a while nothing moved on the bridge. Vasco and his companions were at one end, near the stairs. In the middle were Akar and three other males. On the other side was Olmo, who seemed to have materialized out of nowhere. Only ten or so rats accompanied him.

Regus and Nil waited, holding their breath, for someone to make the first move. But Vasco knew that he had to be first.

"It's Akar who killed your people!" he said to Olmo. "*He* is your enemy!"

Undecided, Olmo looked to one group, then the other. His expression clearly showed what he was thinking: why should he believe Vasco after their terrible fight in the engine room, where many of his most courageous males had been killed?

"We wanted to honor the agreement!" Vasco reminded him. "I told you we were not here to stay. Akar, on the other hand, is here to take revenge!"

Above the bridge, the sky darkened and the rain pattered noisily. The freighter rolled violently. Suddenly lightning illuminated the sky. The rats were startled and grew excited, as if electrified by the furor in the clouds.

"Vasco is a traitor," Akar shouted to Olmo. "The rats that you see with him belong to my tribe. They fled and abandoned us to our death."

Nil spat when she heard this lie.

"Akar is a usurper!" shouted Regus, talking to Akar's three male companions. "He does not deserve to be your leader!"

That was the trigger. Regus, at the height of his anger, leaped forward with his claws out. Right away, Nil also jumped toward Akar. Vasco's heart nearly stopped. In a fraction of a second, Olmo made his decision and entered the fray. He and his companions rushed as one against Vasco's tribe.

Vasco hardly had time to realize the amplitude of the

disaster when claws tore at his back. He rose and started biting at random. On the other side, he could see Akar move directly on Regus to satisfy his revenge.

Vasco cried out. Akar and Olmo were assailing Regus together! Nil managed to escape from her attacker and jumped onto Olmo's back. She tumbled on the ground with him. Using all his weight, Akar fell on Regus and bit his head. Vasco bit those on his left and those on his right in an attempt to come to Regus' rescue. But the black rats blocked his way. He had to eliminate three of them before he could reach the center of the fight.

Regus was standing now. One of his eyes was closed and bloody, but he fought courageously. He managed to push Akar back, while Nil and Vasco continued to claw Olmo.

Around Vasco fighters fell, tumbled, and cried out. Flashes of lightning were now more frequent. The rattling of the rain intensified. Vasco had a wound in his belly. He groaned, he wheezed. When lightning illuminated the bridge, he could see that Regus and Akar were at a standoff. They almost seemed to dance. Their paws slapped the air. They nosed each other. Their blood mingled. Vasco kept on fighting. The black rats prevented him from coming to Regus' aid.

Nil sent out a piercing cry. She was clutching Olmo's fur, gripping his back with all fours. Olmo got up on his hind legs and tried to shake himself free. Nil dug her teeth into his nape and Olmo collapsed. She abandoned him and immediately threw herself on Akar. Akar lost his balance and fell on his side. But he managed to crawl out of sight. Regus was shaken and could hardly stand up.

Just as Vasco was finally able to approach his wounded companion, the whole of Akar's tribe appeared at the end of the bridge. There were about twenty males, strong and heinous, and leading them was Ourga, Akar's horrible and terrifying female. She appeared in all her monstrosity, blood dripping from her nose, as if she had just come from another battlefield.

A deadly silence invaded the bridge. The wounded crawled along the ground. A short truce gave them all a chance to catch their breath. But Vasco knew that everything was lost. He felt as if he were falling into a bottomless hole. His dizziness returned. He looked at all the rats gathered, all of them ready to kill. Their bodies formed an impregnable wall.

A squeak came from the steps leading to the bridge. Vasco dared not turn his head. His eyes were on Ourga alone.

Suddenly Lek jumped onto the bridge and let out a sharp cry. When his eyes met those of Akar, a painful electricity seemed to take hold of him, and his entire body began to spasm.

"Ourga has slaughtered Olmo's tribe!" he shouted. "I saw her! The females, the young ones! They're all dead!"

18

Revenge

Wounded but still able, Olmo stood up. He looked at Lek.

"In the engine room," Lek said. "All dead."

A shiver shot through Vasco's spine. Now was the time! He advanced toward Olmo. Stunned, the old rat of the freighter looked at Ourga. He looked at the blood dripping from her mouth and at her smug expression. At that moment Regus limped forward. He was exhausted, but he glared at Akar and Ourga as if he were looking at barbarians.

One of the black rats of Olmo's tribe suddenly turned about and planted himself by Regus' side. More of them did the same. Olmo was silent. He did not move. He faced Vasco, ready to leap. Vasco tried not to betray any fear. He looked at Olmo without humility.

"We had a contract," he said in a whisper. "In the name of all those who died, I'll honor it."

Enraged, Ourga groaned loudly. The twenty males of her tribe obeyed and advanced together on the bridge. Vasco saw Olmo rise on his hind legs and push back one of Ourga's faithful rats. At last! He had chosen a new side! Hope returned to Vasco. He rushed toward the assailants.

In the middle of the fight, he saw Lek jump onto Akar's back. The skinny rat was fighting his former leader furiously, and the two rolled over the bridge. Vasco couldn't take his eyes off them. He knew that Lek had to settle his account alone.

Akar was already weak. He couldn't run because of his bad leg. He bit at random, without being able to grab his opponent. Lek took hold of his back and looked for his throat. His hind legs clawed Akar's skin. He bit one ear, then the other. Vasco jumped aside to avoid them. His eyes were riveted on this frightful spectacle. He didn't know where he was anymore. He didn't know what was going on around him.

Then Lek let go of Akar and fell back on the bridge. Vasco was about to help him but saw Lek slip under

Akar's belly. And there Lek grabbed his throat. Akar tried to shake him off, uttering weak groans. But Lek's teeth were firmly implanted. He was taking his revenge—and he wasn't about to let go.

Blood ran over Lek's head. Akar staggered over to the edge of the bridge. But there was this weight under him, this humiliated and furious rat who hampered his movements. In the old sewer tribe, Lek had been the submissive and frightened rat who couldn't stand up to Akar. Now, under Vasco's eyes, the situation had reversed itself. Lek tightened his bite with all the rage accumulated in him.

Akar collapsed. Lek remained at his throat despite the risk of being crushed. The leader's paws scratched the floor of the bridge desperately. He hiccupped . . . and then nothing. The tyrant was dead!

Vasco shuddered. With one leap, he was on Akar. He pushed away the rat's huge body and freed Lek. The skinny rat finally let go of his prey. He got up. Blood drooled from his mouth as he looked at Vasco in silent acknowledgment that he had killed Akar and never again would this ghost from the past haunt him. This time Lek had freed himself. He let out a long high-pitched cry. The noise of the ongoing battle reached Vasco's ears again. He saw the flashes of lightning, and the clouds, and Lek standing triumphant in the middle of the chaos.

Mesmerized by this sight, Vasco did not see the blow coming. He didn't have time to react. A terrible pain invaded him, taking his breath away. One of the rats of Akar's tribe had landed on him and planted his teeth at the base of his tail. Fog veiled his eyes. He tried to free himself, to shake off his invisible enemy. He heard muffled cries and groans. More weight was now crushing his abdomen, his thorax. He tumbled and tumbled. . . .

Then somehow he managed to get up on all fours. His enemy lay next to him. He had killed him without being aware of it. He looked around in time to see that Ourga had spotted Akar on the ground and was calling for reinforcements. She rushed at Lek, and though Lek had seemingly been reborn under the thunder of the storm, her attack caught him off guard and she cut his throat with one swipe of her sharp teeth. Lek lay dead on the bridge, his head slumped on Akar's belly.

Ourga had avenged her companion. But she was now alone. Her tribe was beaten. Olmo, Regus, and Nil looked at her in disgust.

The huge female took stock of her loss. She knew that she was trapped. In a desperate move, she darted toward the end of the bridge and disappeared into the dark.

"Regus!" Vasco called.

The two rats took off behind Ourga, leaving the battlefield behind them. Filled with rage, they chased after the rat who had killed Lek, the most faithful one.

19

The End of the Barbarians

The bridge led to another landing, this one deprived of light. Regus and Vasco arrived there just in time to catch a glimpse of Ourga's tail disappearing around the edge of a door. It was so dark that the two rats could rely only on their whiskers and sense of smell. They pushed their snouts past the door. Regus stretched his neck and ambled forward.

"Beware!" Vasco shouted.

Beyond the door was nothing but total emptiness. Disoriented, Vasco listened. Where had Ourga gone? He heard a grating sound and looked above him. A lightbulb went off in his head: this was an elevator shaft. But Ourga couldn't have jumped into the void. She must have found a way to scale the walls.

Vasco extended a paw. He fumbled and finally felt something. Twisting his body, he managed to grab an overhang and haul himself up. He squeaked to encourage Regus to follow him.

Once on the small overhang, the two rats discovered rungs and cables that ran along the wall. Without hesitation, they began their perilous ascent. Their agile paws found supports, which made for a rapid climb. The elevator shaft was long but they could hear Ourga's pants above them, which fueled their anger.

They could make out a light above them too. This light had to be coming through the opening of another door. Ourga seemed to know her way well. Vasco assumed that her tribe had set up camp at the top of the freighter. From there Akar had been able to organize his bloody raids into the belly of the boat. No one would have thought of looking for him so high up.

At last Regus and Vasco reached the opening. They slipped through and found themselves on another landing, this one lit with daylight. Fortunately, no humans were in sight. They sniffed the ground and picked up Ourga's scent. She had run toward the prow of the ship.

Vasco and Regus resumed their chase. A little farther

on they entered a place where a ventilation system was humming, and there they lost Ourga's trace. Akar's female seemed to have vanished. Vasco turned to Regus. The beige rat was panting. A nasty wound had shut one of his eyes. Vasco too felt weak. He had lost blood and his ears were buzzing. Wouldn't it be better to give up? After all, Ourga was alone. She wouldn't be able to attack anyone. She might even die of hunger in one of the nooks of the freighter.

While he pondered these thoughts, Vasco toured the area. It smelled of gasoline and grease. Ducts larger than the ones in the hold opened out toward the top. Vasco thought of Lek. He saw again his triumphant silhouette, could hear again his yell of liberation. He also thought of Joun and her young ones. How was he going to deliver the news of Lek's death?

"There!" Regus said suddenly.

Vasco was startled. He joined Regus in a few leaps. The beige rat had his snout against the larger duct.

"She's in there! I heard the grating of her paws."

Forgetting his doubts, Vasco ran around the duct trying to find a way in. Regus was right—they couldn't give up. Ourga had done too much damage. If he didn't kill her, at least he had to bring her back to face Joun.

On the other side of the duct, Vasco discovered a piece of torn steel. Some bolts were loose and a tiny crack made it possible to enter the duct. Vasco flattened himself and went through the hole first. Regus followed him.

It was as dark as in a tunnel. A draft of cold air rushed in from above. They had entered one of the main exhaust pipes, where all ducts met to spit their fumes out.

Ourga was no longer here. She had probably climbed higher still.

Vasco and Regus began their new ascent with suspicion. The wind swirled around them. The ducts intertwined and formed a sort of complex clump. The two rats skidded. As they climbed, the darkness dissipated. They stopped from time to time to watch for their prey but didn't catch a whiff of her scent. The wind was too strong.

At last, at the very top, Vasco could see the twinkle of red and green lights. With one last effort they would reach the top of the exhaust pipe.

Both rats reached a flange that encircled the pipe near the top. It was windy. An icy dampness penetrated their fur. The pipe resembled a mouth that opened toward the sky. Through the opening, Vasco saw dark clouds merge with the approaching night. Regus came close to him. He was shaking with cold and fear. Pressed up together, the two rats moved on the narrow flange around the exhaust pipe. The noise of the wind, the rain, and the ocean was deafening. At last they discovered

Ourga. She too had reached the top of the pipe. She was trapped. She took a few steps back and curled up on the very edge when she saw Regus and Vasco. She did not seem capable of fighting. She had spent the last of her strength dragging her huge body up here.

Vasco stared at his enemy. What should he do? Plant his teeth in her throat? She looked so miserable.

Buckets of rain fell on the three of them. The gusts of wind were so strong they were losing their balance. They couldn't stay here; it was too dangerous. Regus pushed Vasco toward Ourga.

Vasco hesitated. He had witnessed so many deaths since the beginning of their trip, and he was weary. Ourga's cruelty repulsed him, but Regus pushed him forward once more—he was so close to her now. As he stepped closer still, Ourga looked at him. Her eyes reflected the red flash of the bulbs attached at the edge of the pipe. As Vasco was about to grab her, Ourga cried out. She moved sideways and back—and slipped. Under Regus's and Vasco's eyes, she toppled into the void.

Vasco rushed to the pipe's edge. He saw Ourga falling and falling. . . . Her plunge was from breathtakingly high, but eventually her body crashed on top of the containers lined up on the deck of the freighter.

Vasco leaned over the ocean, unable to take his eyes away from the void. In the dying light that shone across the clouds, he could see Ourga's lifeless body bounce off the containers and tumble toward the rail of the freighter. The wind swept her body, like a dead leaf, into the waves.

The gray sea stretched to the horizon, circling the ship. An intense feeling of sadness mixed with relief invaded Vasco. At the top of the ship, he felt he was flying above the immense sea, under a sky that was turning dark. Yet he was so small and so weak. He was surprised to feel that he belonged to this universe as much as did the ocean and clouds.

"I had doubts about you," Regus told him suddenly. The beige rat, his eyes on the horizon, spoke with confidence. "Now I no longer do. Now you are really our leader."

20

An Orange Peel

Vasco stood in front of Joun and looked at her gravely. The female lay down alongside Lek's body and closed her eyes. Around her, the young ones stood in a silent circle. The rat's dead body was already giving off the dull smell of death.

When he had descended the exhaust pipe a little while ago, Vasco had not gone back to the bridge right away. He had retrieved something that was not heavy yet seemed to weight a ton.

"This is for you," he whispered.

In front of Lek's body, he placed a fragrant orange peel he had gone to find in the garbage in the kitchen.

Joun nosed the orange peel without a word. The rats stayed motionless and silent. They understood Vasco's gesture as a sign of respect, which helped to alleviate their sorrow.

Tiel and Coben rubbed themselves against Vasco. How many dead rats had they encountered since the day Vasco found them on the harbor? Would this nightmare ever end?

Joun looked at all those gathered: Olmo and some exhausted black rats, Regus, Nil, Vasco, and the last survivors of Akar's tribe. Her gaze lingered on each of them, and when she looked at Vasco, he felt a shiver go through him. An immense sadness filled his heart.

"I'm tired," was all that Joun said.

She dragged her feet and crossed over the bridge. Her little ones followed her, their snouts lowered. When they reached the stairs, other rats joined them. They all headed for the large room, now abandoned to darkness. Outside it seemed that the rain had stopped. The swells were calming down and the freighter continued its journey.

One after the other, all the survivors departed from the bridge. They followed Joun in a strange, silent procession as she led them to their new refuge at the prow of the ship. Vasco limped along at the rear. He wondered what the men would think when they discovered all these dead rats in the same spot. They would probably take shovels and bags and toss the corpses into the sea. There, Lek, Akar, and the others would sink to the bottom like small stones, forever united.

21

Land!

A few days later, when Vasco and Regus returned to the shelter with pieces of bread they'd found in the kitchen, they heard the foghorn: three short whistles. Olmo approached them. Although he had survived his wounds, he was definitely weakened by the distressful journey.

"We're going to berth," he announced.

Vasco dropped his piece of bread. Right away, the youngest rats grabbed it, squeaking with pleasure. Their mother, who had given birth in the hold at the beginning of the trip, distributed a few gentle blows to calm them.

She spared only the little female who had nearly died between the jaws of the famished rat, and for whom she cared with special tenderness. Her name was Zeya; she would be blind for life.

"Once the ship is anchored in the harbor, you'll find land again," Olmo went on.

Regus leaped toward Nil at the news. A joyous agitation spread among them. The journey had been so long and so difficult that the news seemed like a ray of sunshine. Vasco was the only one who wondered if more hardship awaited his tribe. He looked at the leader of the black rats.

"Come with us," he told him. "Your tribe was nearly wiped out. Other rats may come on board to take possession of your territory."

Olmo's whiskers quivered. In a glance, he counted the survivors of his tribe—hardly ten. He looked down and rubbed his snout with his paws.

"I've spent my whole life on this ship," he said at last. "I'm old and tired. I'll stay. The others can do whatever they want."

Vasco counted his own flock. What a strange tribe! Since Akar and Ourga's deaths, he had welcomed males from the enemy camp. Now Vasco was leading seventy rats with different scents and different-colored coats. Would he be strong enough to lead them to an unknown land?

Joun joined him. Since Lek's death, the female had lent him precious help, keeping order in the tribe. Everyone obeyed her with respect.

"Olmo will not come with us," Vasco told her. "But the others are free to choose."

Joun nodded. "Let's get ready!"

• • •

The engines of the freighter were humming, and the whole structure vibrated. A strong smell of fuel was in the air. On each deck, men bustled about. They hailed one another, they rushed up, they rushed down, all the while manipulating chains and pulleys. The rats gathered in their shelter and waited silently in the middle of the commotion. Olmo, who was familiar with the noises of the berthing maneuvers, gave them the signal at last. The freighter had docked and was at rest. The entire crew was on the bridge. The rats could hear the screech of cranes and hoisting gears.

For the last time, Vasco guided his tribe through the gangways of the ship. He chose his route with assurance, recognizing the smell of each pipe and landing. As he headed upward, he felt he was leaving a cemetery. Here were the stairs where Hog had been butchered; there was the bridge where Lek had died. A strange nostalgia took hold of him. The freighter had been a nightmarish place, but what would have befallen them had they stayed behind?

Vasco hid his anxiety and kept going up until he reached the stern. Olmo joined him there and guided the group toward daylight.

A bright sunshine flooded the deck outside. The rats were dazzled into motionlessness for a while, their nostrils taking in all the intoxicating outdoor scents. Unknown scents of flowers and spices mingled with the salty smells that they now knew well. Suffocating waves of heat reached them. *We're far away from home,* Vasco couldn't help thinking.

From the top of the rail, he watched the wharf with attention. It was crowded with humans. There were sailors all about, but also a whole population of merchants, women in colorful dresses, and children at play.

There was another presence. Cats!

Attracted by the smell coming from the crates that had been unloaded, the cats crept closer. How many were there? Four, five, six dark shadows appeared from the back of the merchants' stalls. An army of hungry stray cats with arched backs, meowing. Vasco trembled from the tip of his nose to the end of his tail.

From the rail, the rats surveyed with fear the land that they had so longed for. How would they ever be able to leave the freighter?

"You'll make it!" Olmo said. "Try to go this way."

The old rat indicated the cranes and hoisting gear that were unloading the containers. The huge crates swung a moment in the air, turned around and around at the end of their chains, then landed farther down on flatbed railroad cars stationed on the wharf.

Vasco observed the back-and-forth of the cranes, took another look at the cats, then glanced again at the cranes, hesitating. It was risky, but Olmo was offering them the best solution.

"Where is this train going?" he asked Olmo.

"Far away, to the east. I'm sure you'll find refuge there."

Vasco observed the train cars a moment longer, and his eyes followed the straight line of rails. To the east . . . A refuge . . . These simple words transported him to a new world, a new life. A dreamlike life, where cruelty and wars longer existed. A life of peace.

"Let's go," Vasco ordered.

In small groups, the rats wormed their way to the deck. They watched the actions of the humans and those of the pulleys. Olmo and Vasco led each group to the chained containers. At their signal, the rats climbed quickly and crouched on top. Vasco looked on as the containers went up in the sky, swinging dangerously. His heart beat madly. What if they fell? On top of the large crates, the rats clung to the chains. When they landed on the flatbed cars, Vasco sighed with relief.

Several groups left this way until only one remained.

"Come with us!" Vasco said to Olmo once more.

The leader of the black rats shook his head. His whiskers twitched in the breeze. No, he would not come. So Vasco rushed with the last group and climbed onto the container. He could hear the creaking of the chains. He dug his paws in the links. Next to him, Joun wedged herself in a ring, with scared little Zeya between her teeth. A jolt . . . and that was that, as the container left the deck. Vasco held his breath. Below, the sun shimmered brilliantly over the quiet water. Seen from above, the colors of the harbor merged with this magnificent light.

Olmo, alone on board, raised his head and uttered a long cry. Vasco answered him. He was still amazed that this formidable enemy had become a friend.

Vasco was sad but also filled with renewed hope. He wanted to believe that here, in this unknown and fragrant land, he would be able to find a refuge for his tribe.

3

**THE TRIBE
OF THE FOREST**

1

The Train

The sun had reached its zenith and an unrelenting heat pounded the ground, men, and animals like a mantle of lead.

For hours the cargo train had been crawling through a strange landscape where giant trees alternated with vast plains. Vasco and the tribe of rats were gathered on the train, clinging to stay aboard the containers through all the jolts of the journey. Vasco was at the rear, near Joun and the other females. He could hardly breathe, the heat was so humid.

After weeks spent in the hold of the ship, the contrast in climate was harsh. Vasco couldn't help thinking about the dark universe of the ship and its network of gangways, stairs, and ducts. He felt as if he had left a part of himself there. He missed Lek and Hog, whose deaths remained an open wound. As for Akar and Ourga's demise, it brought him little comfort.

A strong jolt suddenly made Vasco lose his balance. His flank knocked against Joun's and he flattened himself instinctively on the top of the container to avoid toppling off. The train ground to a screeching halt. Vasco and Joun raised their heads at the same time. Everything was fine: no one had fallen off. Leaning prudently to the left, Vasco saw a flock of half-starved goats crossing at the front of the tracks. They were guided by children in rags. Joun sighed and gave Vasco a tired look. Would this trip ever end?

Vasco had no answer.

He dreamed of a peaceful refuge and had shared his dream with his companions. He couldn't let them down now.

The train wasn't moving. The little ones weren't complaining too much, and the others patiently endured the discomfort of the ride. But soon hunger was going to invade their stomachs, and they wouldn't find food to satisfy their appetites on this burning container. Vasco took a look at their surroundings; the presence of goats and humans meant that there was a village close by. He was tempted to lead them off the train but changed his mind at the last moment. As far as his eyes could see, the ground was covered with high, dry grass. And it was likely infested with snakes.

"Let's keep going," he told Joun.

Taking advantage of the pause, he walked toward the males in front. Regus' and Coben's eyes seemed to be asking the same questions: *Where are you taking us? How much longer do we have to stay on this roof? What will we discover when we get to our destination?*

Vasco sat with his tail coiled under him. Olmo had seemed confident when he gave them directions. But what did he really know? After all, the old rat had spent his entire life at the bottom of the ship without ever going ashore.

Dogs started barking at the front of the train, and children shouted as they whipped the air with sticks. The flock of goats continued to stretch idly across the tracks.

As if weighed down by the dampness, flies landed on Vasco's coat. He shook himself to chase them away. And what if there was nothing to the east?

"I think we should get off the train here," Regus said suddenly, as if reading Vasco's mind.

The beige rat pointed to the goats with his head. If they followed them, he said, maybe they would reach a village. To survive, the tribe needed to stay close to humans. That was the way they lived, feeding on the trash of humans, whether it was in the sewers of the city, on the harbor, or in the scullery of the freighter.

Coben squeaked to indicate that he agreed with Regus. For some time now, Vasco had felt that he was losing his authority over the young rat. Hog's death had hardened Coben, and he seemed to have forgotten all that Vasco had done for him.

But the train started moving again. All at once Vasco, Regus, and Coben crouched on the container top and tensed their muscles. The rusty frame of the train creaked, the wheels shrieked on the track, and little by little the train gained speed.

"Let's wait some more," Vasco repeated, although he couldn't articulate what he was waiting for.

Regus and Coben didn't protest. They couldn't get off now anyway, since the train was moving too fast. Not far from him Vasco saw Nil curled up, her ears pulled down. He very much wanted to crawl close to her and seek comfort in her company. They had faced much hardship together from the moment they met. They deserved to find a bit of peace and quiet.

As the hot wind penetrated his fur, Vasco looked up. In the distance, he noticed huge curls of black smoke billowing up in the pale sky.

2

The Rebellion

As the wind veered west, it carried the smoke—a mix of burnt plastic, animal grease, excrement, and fumes from exhaust pipes—in their direction. The nauseating smell seized Vasco's throat. His snout between his paws, he closed his eyes. He could hear a brouhaha of human voices, running engines, and honking horns.

The train slowed down. Regus stood up.

"Look!" he whispered to Vasco.

Vasco opened his eyes. He saw the train make its way through an ocean filled not with water but with crude colors, disparate materials, animals, and humans. It was an ocean that rumbled not with the sound of waves but with the noises of a town.

As far as the eye could see there was a mass of shabby wood shacks, crumbling walls, tarps flying in the wind, fabrics, and trash. A jungle of electric wires had sprouted between the shacks. The whole landscape seemed to be swimming in a large muddy puddle, and in the middle of this mess, hundreds of humans milled around. Vasco glimpsed women wearing hats, men armed with picks, others carrying large loads. Farther off in this nightmarish landscape, huge chimneys belched their foul smoke. And here, close to the wheels of the train, Vasco saw dogs as well as an army of stray cats.

So this is what the east holds, he told himself. *It's not a refuge! It's hell!*

Then enticing smells assailed his nostrils. He jumped up. Behind him all the rats inhaled the same odors. No doubt they were coming from the trash piled high between the shacks.

"There's enough food here to feed thousands of rats!" Coben cried, his whiskers quivering with joy.

Vasco felt his heartbeat accelerate. Agitation spread rapidly among the tribe. The young ones started to squeak; they moved away from their mothers as the smells of food acted like a magnet. The males swung their tails nervously. The fever increased as the train made its way through the shantytown. Filled with worry, Vasco was about to go back to Joun when Nil left her spot and jumped in front of him. Drool was hanging from her mouth.

"Let's get off!" she begged. "We're all famished!"

Vasco glanced fearfully at the crowd gathered on each side of the train. Get off? It wasn't possible. Too many cats, too many humans, too many . . . The tribe would be attacked. He looked at Nil and shook his head.

"Much too risky," he said firmly. "We stay here."

The train lumbered on, slowing down even more. A clamor rose from the crowd. Babies were crying, men were shouting, children were throwing stones at the train cars. Vasco suddenly saw a long line of red-furred rats fleeing from a pile of trash, squeaking. In a flash, they disappeared under the wheels of the train, with three or four skinny cats giving chase and meowing frantically. Nil saw them too. Her head down, she seemed resigned to continuing this leg of their journey and returned to the females at the rear of the car. But Coben raised himself on his paws.

"If Nil wants to obey you, good for her—she can die of hunger! But you can't keep me from getting off!" he spat out.

Vasco didn't have time to react. Quick and nimble,

Coben leaped to the head of the car. Immediately Tiel did the same, followed by half a dozen young rats.

"Regus!" Vasco shouted.

The beige rat reacted swiftly. Leaping to Vasco's side, he ran on the heels of the hungry youngsters to try to stop them. But when they both reached the roof of the locomotive, all they could do was look at Tiel and Coben as the two rats disappeared into a pile of half-melted tires.

"Let them go," Regus said, out of breath. "If they get killed, so be it. We tried to warn them."

Vasco shook his head. He couldn't abandon any rat of his tribe in this hellish place. He had already lost Hog on the ship. He refused to lose Tiel and Coben as well. He had to save the last members of his native tribe, whatever the cost.

It was foolish, but his decision was made. He ran to Joun and ordered the tribe to abandon the tops of the containers. Then, leading the group of males, he went back to the locomotive. Regus had already jumped to the ground and was heading for the pile of tires.

"Follow Regus!" Vasco ordered them.

In a few minutes, the whole tribe had deserted the train. When it started to move quickly again, some projectiles grazed Vasco—kids had seen him. He barely had time to slip into a hiding spot.

3

In the Hell of the Shantytown

It was dark under the pile of burnt tires. Vasco's paws sank into a kind of cold glue that stuck to his belly. From the tips of his whiskers, he sensed the curled-up bodies of his companions. Joun had blind little Zeya between her teeth and was surrounded by other females. She raised her neck to deposit Zeya on one of the higher tires, then turned to Vasco for his command.

"Stay here with the weakest ones," he whispered. "I'll bring Tiel and Coben back."

"And something to eat!" she begged.

Vasco nodded and slipped through the tires and shapeless objects piled on the ground. At last he sniffed Regus' scent. The beige rat had managed to gather the males at the other end of the shelter. He had time to glimpse Tiel and Coben and the other young ones as they trotted toward a shack made of planks, a little farther away. Without delay, Vasco designated some of the fastest and most courageous males to accompany him and Regus as they rushed to the shack.

The group passed through disjointed planks and fell onto the other side. Vasco and Regus snooped here and there, unsure of where to go. Some of the males took advantage of the situation and gnawed at pieces of plastic, fabric, and crushed fruit that they ferreted out. The town resembled an open-air sewer.

Vasco finally detected the scent he was looking for. Tiel and Coben were here.

"Let's go," he said, heading straight ahead.

The rats managed to avoid any undesirable encounters and reached a concrete jetty that overhung a marshy expanse. On each side of this pond, filthy accumulations formed a type of unsteady levee. Vasco could hardly believe that Tiel and Coben had wanted to dig their paws in there. Emanations of stagnant water and fish tickled Vasco's nostrils. He moved forward on the jetty, his snout to the ground, following the trace of the young runaways.

Then, suddenly, the noise of a motor attracted his attention. The group stood still, their ears pricked.

"Over there," Regus whispered.

Vasco was startled. He could see a strange little boat crossing the pond in the direction of the jetty. Under a canopy of corrugated iron, a cluster of tightly packed humans were shouting. The motor sputtered and emitted a bluish smoke. Soon the motorboat knocked against the jetty. The men were going to disembark!

"Let's turn around," Regus shouted.

But Vasco noticed shadows moving on the boat's canopy.

"Wait," he ordered.

Tiel and Coben were up there. They had probably climbed to the corrugated roof in the hope of being transported to the trash on the other shore. Vasco squeaked and turned in circles to attract their attention and incite them to return. But he did so in vain.

At the end of the jetty, men began to unload bags. Some of the men were already skipping over the rail of the boat as it got ready to turn back. Without hesitation, Vasco rushed forward. He jumped over the bags, reached the edge of the jetty, and leaped onto the boat. His companions followed, one after the other. Right away, men began to yell. One of them lifted a bag and threw it in front of him to crush Regus. The beige rat nimbly dodged the blow and zigzagged between the legs of the passengers, who yelled more loudly than ever and dealt blows every which way. The motorboat started to pitch. At that moment, Vasco noticed a cable hanging along one of the posts that held up the canopy. He grabbed it with his teeth and planted his claws in the nylon. Twisting his back, he managed to climb to the roof along this improvised ladder.

He hardly had time to find his balance when he felt the roof vibrate under his paws. The men had discovered the group of rats who had taken cover there and they started throwing bags and cans to chase them off. Panicked, Tiel and Coben took refuge near Vasco, who had retreated to the edge of the canopy. His paws had no grip. The boat was pitching, and if the men continued to throw bags, the roof was going to collapse. Vasco leaned over the canopy. Thick, dark water stared back at him.

Suddenly a bag smashed down on top of one of the young males, immobilizing him. Vasco looked at him desperately. One of the men on the jetty grabbed a long stick and hit the roof, trying to knock off any rat he could.

Vasco used his snout to push Tiel and Coben toward the edge.

"Jump!" he shouted. He was the first to hurl himself overboard.

The cold water slapped his body, entering his nose

and ears. He swam vigorously to come back to the surface. When his head emerged from the water, he saw that Tiel and Coben were swimming in front of him with all the strength of their young muscles. His snout at water level, Vasco sliced through the slick water, moving away as fast as possible from the motorboat. When he thought he was a safe distance away, he looked back. In the slight ripples, he could see that a dozen rats were following him. The only missing rat was the one who had gotten pinned under the bag. His back had been broken and he could not escape.

At last, the group reached the opposite shore. Vasco joined Tiel and Coben, who were resting on top of rotten cardboard boxes.

"You nearly got all of us killed!" he scolded as the young rats shook and licked their oily coats.

Coben didn't pay attention to him. He continued to clean his paws. As for Tiel, she squeaked with satisfaction, explaining how she had nibbled the remains of a bird skeleton before ending up on the boat. She showed Vasco a smoking pile of trash at the edge of the pond.

"It was here. But I ate it all."

Vasco approached her, his fur all bristled. He could not believe that while he had been risking his life to look for them, Tiel and Coben had been feasting.

"What about the others?" he hissed. "The females,

the young ones? Did you think about bringing them any food?"

Coben stopped licking his paws and looked up. "They can help themselves! There's plenty of food to go around!"

As Vasco arched his back, Regus leaped between him and Coben and looked straight into Vasco's eyes. With his own he seemed to say, *Why start a fight? There are other priorities! Coben is young and impetuous. He will learn to care about the needs of the entire group later on in life.*

Vasco sighed. "Let's go back to the pile of tires," he said, willing himself to stay calm.

Nevertheless, he gave Coben an angry swat.

"Bring back something for Joun," he ordered him. "If you don't, you can look for another tribe."

4

The Council of Rats

When the rats finally reached the pile of tires, it didn't look the same as before. Some tires had fallen from the top, while others had rolled down to the bottom of an embankment. Fear knotted Vasco's stomach: he had just seen the lifeless body of a young female under one of the tires. Vasco and Regus looked at one another. Something must have happened while they were away. Gingerly they inspected the surroundings and sniffed the ground. Vasco stopped when he detected a strong smell of urine. Cats!

The blood in his veins froze. He rushed under the

tires expecting to find the partially eaten bodies of his tribe. But as he advanced farther in the dark, he didn't encounter anything, either dead or alive.

As he came out of the deserted shelter, he heard Coben cry out in the midst of a concert of sharp squeaks. Then he saw Joun and the young ones emerge from a pile of bricks, pushing and shoving to share the bread crusts and fish head that Coben had brought them. Nil broke from the group and rushed over to Regus. A long red scratch adorned her left flank.

"Three stray cats!" she said. "They smelled our presence and attacked us several times."

Vasco could hear her irregular breathing. The female turned to him.

"They caught two females," she added, shaking. "I managed to get the others out."

Vasco looked at Nil's flank. Drops of blood oozed down her brown fur. He was about to lick her wound, but Regus pushed him back with a little pat.

"It's my job," he said.

Nil lay down on her side and let Regus tend to her with obvious relief. Vasco stepped back. As he looked at them, he felt a sharp pain in his chest, as if an invisible foe were piercing his heart.

With effort, he walked toward the pile of bricks. The mud drying on his chest had hardened like an oppressive crust. Around him, groups of men in rags came and went with indifference. The entire town sank and baked under the sun, yet Vasco was cold. He flattened his snout on the ground, feeling dizzy.

The tribe is on the wrong track, he thought.

He buried his whiskers in the mud. His thoughts were clearer now: looking for proximity to humans was not the way to find shelter. Although the men here did not seem intent on exterminating the rat population, what kind of life would the tribe have among all this refuse? Each day the cats would destroy one of them. Each day they would have to face danger, rebuild a nest, kill or be killed.

"Let's move out of here," he said suddenly.

He got up, shook himself, and ran toward Joun. The old female was helping Zeya find a spot among the rats gathered around the fish. Vasco shoved aside the other females and leaped excitedly toward Joun.

"Let's move out of here!" he repeated. "Help me convince the others!"

Joun didn't even glance at him. She held Zeya between her paws and kept pushing her forward.

"Did you hear me, Joun?" Vasco said, irritated. "We have to flee! We narrowly escaped the slaughter! I refuse to settle for this type of future!"

Vasco turned in frustrated circles as Joun stayed impassive and kept guiding the young blind rat. Finally

Vasco stood still and watched little Zeya worm her way through a forest of tails and paws. She gave small, timid blows left and right, silent but determined. In spite of her handicap, she managed to find a spot in the crowd, and when she finally grabbed a piece of flesh between her teeth, Joun squeaked to congratulate her.

"This little one will have a hard time surviving," the old female said. "She can't ever be left alone."

Vasco watched Zeya a little longer. He remembered the locked hold of the freighter, the fury of the hungry males who had hurled themselves on the newborns to eat them. Zeya had almost perished.

"I'll take care of her," he told Joun, coming out of his reverie. "But we have to leave this awful place."

"Where would we go?" she wanted to know.

"I'm not sure," Vasco confessed. "Far away. Lek would agree with me if he were still alive."

Joun seemed responsive to this argument, for Lek had admired Vasco's courage and undoubtedly would have followed him.

Nil and Regus now entered the space under the pile of bricks, and Vasco informed them of his decision.

"You're saying we should go away from the town and its humans?" Regus said in disbelief, swinging his tail.

Coben, who had overheard the conversation, spoke up. "Why?" he asked.

Other young rats gathered around Vasco, while Joun collected the females.

"If we organize ourselves," Coben went on, "we can have a good life here! I saw tons of fresh garbage arrive in trucks when I was on the other side of the pond."

"It's true!" Tiel confirmed. "It's all there for the taking and—"

"And then what?" Vasco cut her off sharply. "Eat, kill, or die. Is that all you're interested in?"

Silence fell on the group. Vasco reared in the middle, trying to keep his cool and appear tall and strong. If he wanted to convince them, he had to look sure of himself.

"We've always lived at humans' expense," he said. "So far it's brought us only desolation and death. Try to remember why we left the harbor . . . and the sewers."

From the corner of his eye, he saw that Regus and Nil were in agreement. The memories of the town were still firmly engraved in their minds. Vasco knew that he had just hit the bull's-eye. For the first time in a long while, he thought of Memona. She embodied the memory of the tribe and all its wisdom. Vasco remembered what she had told him of long-ago times when rats lived in the wilds of nature. These ancestors had managed to feed themselves without the presence of humans. Why couldn't that be possible again?

"We have to invent another way of life!" Vasco added

firmly. "We must go away and discover a place that will be a real refuge. A place that offers more than mere survival. A place where we can truly live and thrive."

Once more Nil and Regus seemed to agree. As he saw his authority reinforced, Vasco turned to the females, awaiting their verdict. He knew that the whole tribe would follow if the females rallied around him.

Joun stood up in the center of the circle. "We have thought it over!" she announced. "The females fear for the lives of their little ones in this place. There must be something better farther east. So Vasco is right: let's leave."

5

A Smell of Soil and Bark

The day was waning. Here and there, lights flared up in the shantytown. At the foot of electric poles, children kicked old cans around as they shouted, and men pulled on wires to link their shacks to improvised outlets. Radio sets were chattering. The smell of fires floated in the air. It was the hour when cats meowed and babies cried.

Leaving the pile of bricks behind, Vasco led his tribe beyond the embankment of the railroad track. He chose to follow the track, hoping to find the train again. The rats trotted silently behind him. One after the other, they jumped over the sleepers, their whiskers quivering, attentive to the slightest sign of danger. Regus and Nil brought up the rear. By his side, Vasco felt the restive presence of Tiel and Coben, whom he had ordered not to wander off under any pretext. The two young rats were under tight watch following their afternoon escapade. Vasco knew that he couldn't afford to make a mistake: if they didn't find the train, if they didn't leave the shantytown this very evening, no one would ever trust him again.

Night came on fast but the heat was still stifling. The soil was warm under Vasco's paws. He sniffed as he moved on, zigzagging between the rails. On each side of the embankment, on the slopes of trash, other rats foraged and fought.

Suddenly a wooden fence barred the way. Vasco approached it, slipped underneath and squeaked. The railroad track stopped here! Vasco walked back and turned to his companions. No more rails meant no more train!

"Let's go back!" Coben immediately suggested. "You made a mistake. We should have stayed where we were!"

Vasco ignored his remark and disappeared again behind the fence. His snout to the ground, he explored the surroundings. He was on an uneven asphalted surface where weeds were growing. Looking up, he made out the imposing shape of factory chimneys emitting their greasy fumes above the shantytown. Farther away, he discovered containers and remnants of train cars standing on their chassis. He was about to rejoin the others when he heard human voices. He moved in their direction and noticed red lights piercing the night. The rear lights of trucks! Very carefully, Vasco ran along the rusty cars. Several vehicles were stationed there, not far from the railroad tracks. Men were checking the fastenings of the trailers with flashlights. Vasco took a few leaps closer to sniff the air. Odors of soil and vegetation wafted from the trailers. Their wheels were covered with a thick coat of mud that smelled of clay, slime, and mold.

At that moment, the men turned off the flashlights and the truck engines started up. Vasco shuddered. These odors vaguely reminded him of gardens after the rain. With a bit of luck, the trucks would leave town for a wilder spot. As quick as lightning, he rushed back to his companions and with an imperative squeak ordered them to follow him.

The whole group rushed toward the trucks.

"Faster!" Vasco shouted. "Climb under the tarps!"

The engines were all running now. Doors were slamming. Departure was imminent. Leaping on the step at the back, the most vigorous males opened the way. Joun, Regus, and Nil pushed the young ones on board in a hurry, while Vasco grabbed a young female between his teeth and in turn jumped on the rear of the trailer.

As the truck started moving, Vasco took a look around. The whole tribe had had time to climb aboard. In the red trail left by the rear lights, the shantytown disappeared. The black chimneys, the shacks, the meows, the mountains of trash—all the animal and human chaos melted in the dark.

Vasco's pounding heart calmed down. He could hear the crunching and grating of his companions around him and searched out Nil and Joun.

"Look," the old female told him.

The floor of the truck was covered with bark, along with tender and fragrant wood chips. The young rats pounced on them and tried to extract the fibers with their sharp teeth. The older ones foraged in the sawdust to find worms or dead insects that had fallen from branches. For the time being, at least, the tribe was not going hungry.

• • •

In the early morning Vasco was awakened by the violent jolts of the vehicle. He got up quickly. The other rats woke up too. Humid daylight seeped through the opening of the tarp, as well as strong and unfamiliar smells. Vasco slipped, tried to plant his claws in the floor, rolled on his side, then slid toward the rear. The females and young ones crouched on their paws in an attempt to maintain their balance, but the jolts worsened, sending the rats in all directions.

Finally the vehicle stopped at a tilted angle. The rats caught their breath. Vasco glanced toward an opening in the tarp and saw large patches of something green waving in the wind.

"I've never smelled anything like this before," he said.

Human voices broke the silence outside. Apparently the convoy of trucks had reached its destination. Regus and Vasco pushed their snouts through the tarp. A light fog covered the landscape, yet the heat was already as oppressive as a furnace. The wheels of the truck were half sunken in muddy yellow soil. All around the clearing where the trucks had stopped, giant trees formed a green crown. Suddenly a concert of strident engines started up, chasing birds to higher branches.

"Chain saws!" Regus whispered. "I heard this racket once before, in a sawmill near the harbor!"

Men now appeared not far from the truck. They lifted the tarp of another vehicle.

"We can't stay put," Regus said. "They'll come to our truck soon!"

Vasco noticed fallen rocks a few steps away. He turned to his companions.

"Follow me!" he ordered.

6

The Clearing

The tribe was hardly out of the truck when a noise
pierced the air. It started with a sinister snap, followed by
a whistle, then by a heavy impact that shook the ground.
Vasco and his companions looked at each other fearfully.
Their nostrils flared and their whiskers quivered.

Then silence returned, as intense as the noise itself.
Vasco looked up toward the sky. There was not a bird in
sight, not a sign of life. Suddenly the noise of the chain
saws started again, a sound that resembled the buzzing of
a swarm of wasps.

"So this is your refuge?" Coben asked as he approached the heap of rocks.

The young rat climbed over some collapsed stones and positioned himself at the top. Vasco watched him with suspicion. The young rat he knew had become a strong and proud male who might one day be a source of problems for him. Coben would always have the support of his sister, Tiel, as well as of many of the younger ones. But as long as Regus and Vasco stayed united, the tribe would follow them.

"Vasco led us here," Coben said, "but he doesn't know this place! Look around you. There is no refuge."

The other rats grew fidgety. The damp atmosphere, the buzzing of the chain saws, and the presence of men did not instill confidence.

"We still have time to go back where we came from!" Coben went on. "All we have to do is board the truck and wait until it goes in the opposite direction."

At that moment, the engines of the trucks started again. Vasco was startled. The wheels skidded in the wet ground, sending sprays of mud in the air. The splatterings fell down close to the rats, who scattered, squeaking loudly. Fortunately Regus brought them back in line.

The trucks finally heaved themselves out of the mud and moved slowly away, deeper into the clearing. Vasco saw a group of men loaded with equipment head in their direction. He sent a warning cry and slipped under the rocks that Coben had used as a pulpit a moment ago. The others imitated him.

The men settled a few steps away, at the foot of a huge tree with a smooth gray trunk. They unrolled cables and placed helmets on their heads, then grabbed their tools. Metallic blades glistened in the first rays of the sun. Fascinated and terrified, Vasco watched them from his hiding place between the rocks. The other rats also looked at what was unfolding.

One of the men started his chain saw. Amid the deafening noise, he sank the blade into the bottom of the trunk. Wood chips spurted around him like a cloud of mad insects. Vasco could feel the vibrations of the electric machine deep down in his flesh.

When he finished, the man stepped back, turned off his saw, and shouted loudly to his companions. The workers started pulling on cables. Vasco put his snout out and looked at the top of the tree. It wavered a second, then with a long cracking sound it slewed to one side and came tumbling toward the ground.

Vasco jumped back and shouted just as the tree crashed down a few meters away from their shelter. A jumble of branches covered the rocks, having missed the tribe by a hair. A cloud of sawdust invaded the confined hiding place, going up the rats' nostrils. Vasco was suffocating. He scratched at the air with his paws and managed to get out of the pile of rocks. Nil leaped by his side, frightened. From all directions, Vasco heard the squawking of the young ones and the females searching for them in the rubble. Luckily, only secondary tree limbs had fallen on their refuge. All the young ones huddled together.

"Men are destroying the forest! Men are destroying the forest!" they whispered to one another, clearly stunned.

Vasco now understood why the sky and clearing seemed so empty and lifeless—animals had fled this place. For Vasco's tribe, lingering here was out of the question.

"We have to move farther on!" Vasco shouted. "Right now!"

Leaving no time to the others to ponder his decision, Vasco rushed into the forest, following a path that was thick with giant ferns. His instinct told him that this was the best direction to go. So, as fast as he could, his nostrils still filled with sawdust, he left the clearing behind.

The rats of the tribe followed him. They too heard the noise of the chain saws starting up again, and understood that other trees would be felled and come crashing down. Even Coben did not protest, but swiftly moved along with the rest of the group, his ears flat against his nape.

Vasco could feel the stems of the ferns slap his back.

His paws slipped on the damp, mossy carpet that covered the undergrowth. The smell of dirt gradually disappeared and was replaced by the more complex scents of tropical vegetation. The farther the rats progressed into the jungle, the darker it got. Soon the canopy of trees was so dense that only a few rays of light passed through. It was almost like nighttime.

Yet Vasco didn't slow down. He knew how to navigate in the dark. The obscurity of the sewers had been a favorite of his in the past. But that world was behind him now, and he adapted his movements to the jungle, a place teeming with protruding roots as well as decomposing leaves, fallen twigs, and rocks that stuck out on the otherwise soft forest floor. A kind of intoxication spread within him as he ran. At long last he was treading on the new land that he had so much hoped for.

But now that the buzzing of the chain saws had died, Vasco sniffed another kind of danger. He slowed down. Behind him he heard the breathing of his companions, and in front he heard the noise of running water.

"What's the matter?" Nil asked as she came up alongside him.

Vasco stood up behind a curtain of ferns. Up ahead, a river was blocking their way.

7

Deep in the Jungle

For a long while Vasco guided the tribe along the river-bank. Sometimes the rats followed the slimy clay edge, which hampered their progress; sometimes they veered off course because the tree roots protruded so high that they formed an impassable barrier. Exhaustion and tension kept them silent. They trotted side by side in tight formation as strange shrieks exploded from the top of the forest, answered by other mysterious screeches. Birds, monkeys, and other faceless fauna haunted the place.

Whenever he could, Vasco observed the river and

wondered whether they should try to cross it. On the opposite bank, the vegetation seemed slightly less dense. Sandbars advanced into the water and the sun managed to reach the ground, giving the shore a more welcoming aspect.

Regularly Joun ran up to the front of the file to trot by Vasco's side. She touched him with the tips of her whiskers, waiting to be reassured. Behind each shrub, trunk, or root, a predator might be watching. How would they be able to fight invisible and unknown enemies?

Suddenly a dark moving mass appeared on the river. Vasco ordered his group to stop. As the mass came closer, he could see that it consisted of tree trunks attached by cables, and that it slid with the current of the river. Men probably used this means of transportation to send the cut wood downstream.

Vasco looked around him. In this part of the jungle, it was useless to look for a refuge. He observed the trunks that butted each other on the water. If they swam fast enough, they should be able to reach them. His companions were dead tired after this long and painful march, but they had to give it a try.

"Do as I do!" he shouted, immediately cannonballing into the dark water.

As he resurfaced he saw Nil, Regus, and Joun still on the bank, petrified. Then they rushed to the edge and watched Vasco swim to the middle of the river. Understanding his intentions, they looked at each other questioningly. Would the weakest ones be able to reach the trunks?

Nil was the first to make a decision. She had followed Vasco through far more dangerous situations, so crossing this river must not have seemed so daunting. To embolden the others, she grabbed a young male in her mouth and jumped into the water.

Soon all the rats dove in behind her. Before she jumped, Joun put Zeya in the care of Regus, and cautioned him to be particularly attentive. Regus then advanced slowly into the mud and began to move his paws, his neck held high, making sure that the snout of the blind little one stayed above water.

In the meantime, Vasco had reached the closest trunk. He planted his claws in the bark and hauled himself out of the water. Dripping, he turned and sighed with deep relief when he saw Nil approaching the trunk. He bent down and delicately lifted the young rat in Nil's charge. When Nil was by his side, he rubbed himself against her to warm her up.

Moments later, the whole tribe was gathered on the trunks. The current wasn't too strong, so the rats sat on their tails and licked their paws.

Leaving Zeya in the care of the females, Regus joined Vasco and Nil.

"We can't turn around anymore." He sighed. "The trucks are too far from us now."

Nil shivered as she curled up against Regus. "I hope you know what you're doing," she said, looking at Vasco.

Vasco did not answer; he turned his eyes to the sandy bank. Ever since witnessing the extermination of hundreds of his own kind by men, he had known that the future of his tribe was compromised. Exile and isolation seemed to be the only solution, but this jungle was unlikely to be a peaceful haven. The air was saturated with insects and hostile clamors. Surely numerous dangers awaited them. He knew that Nil, Regus, Joun, and the others were aware of it too.

As if to confirm his fears, a grunting noise sounded in the undergrowth. Vasco pricked up his ears. Branches were moving near the bank. A second later, a big animal with a long snout dashed out of the bushes. Although the rats were out of its reach, Vasco backed up. It was definitely advisable to stay on the raft.

The river carried them smoothly between rows of huge trees, and they all took advantage of this respite to gather their strength. Only as night fell did the rats come out of their torpor.

Now that the sun had sunk behind the trees, the river took on shades of gray and blue, and clouds of insects flew over its surface. The noises of the jungle had changed. On the banks, toads were gathering, and birds, attracted by the insects, grazed the raft with strident shrieks. Vasco immediately sensed that anxiety was creeping over his companions. Coben and Tiel complained of hunger, which made the other young rats clamor for food as well.

"Let's not stay here!" Nil begged. "We must find a shelter for the night."

The meanderings of the river started to narrow. On one of the banks, Vasco noticed some flat rocks, and behind them tree trunks laden with large brown fruit. Right away, he ordered the females to gather the little ones at the rear, and on his signal they all abandoned the raft.

8

Change of Habits

It was pitch dark in the undergrowth. Vasco's whiskers, his sense of smell, and his ears were his only guides.

"Imagine that you're in the sewers," he told his companions to reassure them.

Yet a diffuse anguish wrung his heart. He knew that nighttime predators were the most dangerous. Snakes, in particular, slid noiselessly toward their prey. . . . Vasco shivered as he remembered the viper that had attacked a young rat lost in one of the empty lots of the industrial area near the harbor. In a second he had been struck down by the venom. Here in the wild, deadly species must abound.

The immense jungle was filled with moans and whistles. Vasco heard the frenetic flapping of wings in the branches, along with strange barkings, as if flying dogs had elected to inhabit the canopy. As he approached the fruit-bearing trees that he had noticed from the raft, he suggested that the tribe set up camp for the night.

Regus and the other males, who had also noticed the appetizing smells, gathered around the trees. The fruit was attached to the trunks like a garland. As Regus attempted to climb by hanging on to creepers, Vasco hurried to join the huddled females, who arched their backs, attentive to the slightest noise. The moss and ferns exhaled a musky perfume that aroused the instinctive suspicion of the rats. It wouldn't be long before nocturnal predators left their burrows to hunt. The tribe had to find shelter in a hurry.

"There's nothing here to make a nest," Joun said, sounding worried. "The bark and dead leaves don't offer enough protection!"

Vasco darted among the females as he sniffed the moss, mushrooms, dead wood, stones, and mud on the forest floor.

"We have to dig into the ground," he said to Joun. "It's the only way."

Cries of protest exploded. The females who had lived on the freighter with Olmo had never dug anything in their lives. They had never used their claws other than to fight.

As the young ones began to cry, Nil stood up. Encouragingly, she reminded them that Akar's tribe had dug a nest under the apartment building, behind the garbage room. Joun couldn't have forgotten that she too had lived in those underground corridors. They had to use their past experience and do the same thing here.

"If the males help us," Nil added, "we'll soon be secure."

The females kept quiet. In the dark, their eyes gleamed like polished stone. Nil was right—they didn't have a choice. If they wanted to keep their young ones out of reach of wild animals, they had to dig.

At that moment, Regus let out a sharp cry. All the females were startled. Vasco rushed in the direction of the tree.

"Look, Vasco!" Regus shouted. "Up here!"

Vasco looked above him and scrutinized the darkness. One meter off the ground, Regus was swinging from a creeper. He had succeeded in cutting the stems with his teeth, and several fruits had toppled onto the ground. The males rushed joyously on the bounty.

The females and young ones in turn threw themselves

at this food fallen from heaven. After desperate efforts, Tiel and Coben succeeded in piercing the fruit's hard shell. The sucking noises that he heard around him made Vasco realize that his empty stomach was cramping. He had not eaten all day!

The flesh of the fruit was firm under his sharp teeth. Then a totally new taste invaded his mouth. The fruit was bland and rubbery, almost impossible to chew. Vasco let go of it to clean his snout. A sticky substance clung to it. He suspected it would harden and paralyze his whiskers.

"We won't survive on this," Nil said, hitting the brown shell with her paw.

One by one, the disappointed rats abandoned the fruit.

Night was coming on and alarming noises increased in the undergrowth. It was time to get to work. Vasco explained to the males what was expected of them. But participating in nest building made them grumble.

"It's the work of the females!" Coben protested. "Males never build nests."

"Except in cases of emergency!" Vasco pointed out. "We're no longer in the city. We have to change our way of life."

Vasco looked to Regus for support, but the beige rat walked off from the group.

"I'll be more helpful hunting," he muttered. "Since the fruit isn't edible, I'll look for insects."

Coben rushed over to him, along with a large number of the young males. Vasco sighed in resignation when he heard them slip away through the bushes.

"You're letting them go?" Nil said indignantly.

Vasco knew that Nil would have preferred to join Regus, but he shook his head. What could he do against them? The beige rat had always been solitary and rebellious. He never obeyed anyone. His joining the tribe when they abandoned the city had been unexpected. The problem was that he wasn't the best role model for Coben. Vasco once again thought of Lek. The skinny, frightened rat had been a faithful ally. He never would have refused to help the females dig. But Regus didn't possess clan spirit.

"At least he'll bring back some food!" Vasco said.

Quickly forgetting his grudge, he started to dig with his front paws. Nil ended up joining him, while Joun and the others united their efforts to dig a second hole. Soon a two-way tunnel took shape under the roots of a fig tree.

With dirt in his eyes and his ears, Vasco was intent on enlarging the bottom of the tunnel. By his side, Nil didn't spare her energy. She scraped furiously, throwing the dirt outside. To shelter the whole tribe, spacious nooks and crannies had to be laid out, otherwise the rats would suffocate.

As he stuck his head outside to catch his breath, Vasco caught a whiff of an unknown smell. His heartbeat sped up. This potent and beastly odor was not friendly. He looked up . . . and saw two shiny eyes at the foot of the roots, staring right at him.

9

The Beast

Vasco sent an alert signal that had all the females scurrying with the little ones into the tunnel. But the males who had not gone hunting with Regus couldn't find room in the unfinished burrow. Vasco could hear them squeaking outside. If they didn't find shelter, the beast would devour them.

In the tunnel, it was pandemonium. The ground caved in in spots, closing the way, and Vasco was busy clearing the clods to avoid suffocation.

"There are too many of us!" Joun cried. "The whole structure will collapse."

"Let's dig deeper!" Nil suggested.

As she got to work, other females enlarged the nest and clods of dirt flew amid the frightened squeaks of the young ones. Nil gnawed as fast as she could at the roots that obstructed the way. Vasco looked at her with admiration. She and Joun were perfectly capable of finishing the job. He would go up to try to find Regus and Coben . . . if they weren't already dead.

Jumping over the little ones, he hurried up. He sniffed the ground and air before sticking his head out. The beast smell was gone. But Vasco could hear some soft cries, groans, and squeaks of rats. Maybe wounded ones were calling? He rushed out of the tunnel.

"Ah! Here comes the leader!" Regus exclaimed when he saw Vasco appear.

Vasco stopped in disbelief. The hunters had returned, and the males were quietly seated, sharing the corpse of a huge spider, along with that of several hairy insects.

"Where's the beast?" Vasco inquired.

He looked up at the tree branches. The beast's eyes had been shiny like those of a cat, but the creature was not a cat. He was sure of that. Only a moment ago, it had been ready to eat him!

An old male from Olmo's tribe came near Vasco with a dead insect in his mouth. It was a bug as impressive in size as the spider. He dropped it in from of him.

"What you saw wasn't an enemy," he said. "It was a hoofed animal and it took off when it heard your shouts."

Vasco sighed with relief and felt ashamed to have panicked for so little reason. Near the roots of the fig tree, Coben, Regus, and the others were licking their mouths contentedly. This was a good sign. If the males realized that they could find food in the jungle, they might be more willing to settle here.

Vasco grabbed the insect the old male offered him, pushed it in the hole, and went back near the females to give them their share of food.

The corpse of the insect had hardly made its way down the tunnel when a group of famished young rats rushed to it. The carapace that protected the bug's abdomen snapped under their teeth, and the females fought over the legs and head. Vasco looked for Zeya to help her find her way between the others. When he was sure that she would get her share, he moved farther into the tunnel to find Nil.

"You can stop digging," he told her. "Everything is fine. Regus brought back some food."

Nil emerged from the depth of the burrow, her snout covered with dirt. She looked exhausted but seemed especially happy to know that Regus was alive. Although Vasco knew that the young female had become attached to the beige rat, he felt a sting of jealousy each time he had proof of it.

"This nest will be good enough for the night," Nil

said as she followed Vasco to the top. "We'll consolidate it tomorrow."

They followed a sloping tunnel, and as they were about to get out, clods of dirt descended upon their heads. In a sudden confusion, all the males rushed inside at the same time. Nil and Vasco moved back in a hurry, smelling the scent of fear that emanated from their companions.

"Another animal!" shouted one of the terrified males. "A dangerous one."

The whole tribe was now packed into the narrow nest. An untidy heap of bodies, tails, and paws intermingled at the risk of having the roof of the tunnel collapse. At the end of the gallery, Regus' head appeared. Nil and Vasco slipped toward him, pushing and shoving the others without consideration.

"The beast arrived on us noiselessly!" Regus whispered. "It looked like a weasel but its head was black. Two of us were killed!"

Vasco stood abruptly and squeaked furiously, "Where is Coben?"

Regus winced. "Coben? I don't know. I didn't have time to—"

Vasco cut him short. Instinctively he hurled himself straight ahead.

When he neared the exit, he heard squeaks. He felt a

presence. Half of Coben's body was inside, the other half was outside. Vasco approached him and soon figured out that the young male had his teeth planted in the body of the giant spider and was trying desperately to drag it inside the burrow. But outside, the beast groaned and pulled feverishly in the opposite direction. It was a tug-of-war, and the beast was very likely stronger than Coben.

"Let it go!" Vasco shouted. He gave a blow to Coben's back.

"No!" Coben huffed. "I'm hungry! I won't give my prey to someone else!"

Suddenly the body of the spider broke in two and Coben fell back with the lower part of the bug between his paws. Outside, the animal snarled aggressively and shoved its nose into the opening. Its jaws snapped in the void. Terrified, Vasco backed away and pulled Coben toward the end of the tunnel. The beast finally withdrew its head and moved off.

"A little longer and it would have gulped you down with the spider," Vasco told Coben. "You should be a lot more conscious of danger!"

Coben shook himself. The sour scent of fear that enveloped him signaled that he had had the fright of his life. Vasco gave him a little scratch on the ear. The young male's attitude exasperated him, but he resented Regus even more. The beige rat was free to take all the risks he wanted on his own, but that didn't give him the right to incite Coben to do the same.

Coben gave Vasco a vexed look, then ran to the center of the hole to join the others.

His back against the wall of the tunnel, Vasco caught his breath.

This first day in the jungle had gotten the best of him. Would the tribe get used to this new environment? Had he made a good choice by leading the tribe to this place? These unanswered questions reinforced his feeling of loneliness and made him nostalgic. His life would have been so simple if men had not killed his family. He would have been happy to be a rat among other rats, to eat and sleep without having to suffer for the sake of others.

10

The Vagrant of the Trees

Life got organized during the following days. Vasco was relieved that the most reticent males seemed to accept this new way of living, far from men and their trash. Under Regus' command, they hunted in small groups as soon as daylight broke through the foliage. They brought back mostly insects, but some experimented with what they found growing around the entrance to the burrow—mosses, roots, wild berries—or anything else they could find.

In the meantime, the females improved the burrow. They dug new tunnels to create nooks where each litter of rats could have its own nest. Multiple exits were created in case an enemy penetrated inside.

On the third day, Vasco returned to the burrow and discovered one of the young males from Olmo's former tribe lying near a partly eaten mushroom. He was dead. His body was shriveled and a bluish drool covered his mouth. Vasco gathered the tribe around the body so that they could all sniff the deadly mushroom and thus avoid it in the future.

In this fashion, the memory of the rats enriched itself with an array of dangerous signals new to them, including the musky smell of the civet cats who came out at night only; the more discreet smell of the weasels who surged out of holes under tree roots; the sharp leaves of some ferns that could notch your back when you ran under them; the singular hiss of tree snakes; the droppings left by nocturnal birds of prey; and the poison of white mushrooms.

Constant vigilance was necessary, but Vasco grew increasingly confident. Life in the jungle seemed to agree with the females. Several of them were expecting, and soon the tribe would be large enough to ensure future generations.

Taking advantage of these relatively peaceful times, Vasco went for long solitary expeditions, penetrating deeper into the forest each day. In this dark and luxuriant immensity, trees stretched up to a sea of azure blue. Vasco looked up and saw the sky peer through the leaves. Creepers and strange fruit hung from the trees, shaken now and then by howling monkeys, flying squirrels, and hook-beaked birds. Vasco felt strangely attracted to the universe that flourished above his head, as well as to its dizzying heights.

Like all members of his species, Vasco had a great sense of balance. His claws allowed him to hang on to the bumps and rough spots of tree trunks. But he lacked the skill and endurance to go too far up. The natural habitat of the rat was never far from the ground . . . yet Vasco was determined. At first he chose to train on an uprooted fig tree that had fallen over other trees and formed a bridge sloping upward. As he persevered, Vasco slowly acquired new reflexes. The muscles of his legs grew stronger, his fear decreased, and after several tumbles, he learned to keep his balance and avoid falling.

Once he reached the high branches, Vasco felt intoxicated. He tasted the fruit and the sap of the stems, and he hid under the leaves to watch the dance of the gibbons.

These discoveries brought solace to his solitude since he felt alienated from the tribe's life. He couldn't share the pleasure of roaming in the trees with any other rat. Joun was kept busy by the females and the expected babies. Nil and Regus were always together, and Tiel and

Coben were now completely independent. Only blind little Zeya sought out Vasco's company. He often encountered her on his path.

"Teach me how to climb the trees," she requested one day.

"How do you know that I climb?" Vasco asked, shaking his head. He didn't think that a young blind rat could survive the dangers lurking in the foliage. "Stay with Joun," Vasco told her. "You're too weak to come with me."

"I recognize our enemies as well as you do," Zeya protested. "I can hear a snake approach from the other end of the jungle!"

Vasco remained intractable. He pushed Zeya gently away with his snout and slipped behind the bushes without turning back.

He trotted in the direction of the uprooted fig tree, wormed his way under the roots, jumped, and climbed up to the fork of a large branch. There he stopped, his senses on the alert. Over the usual rustling of birds, he detected distant cracking noises, accompanied by a continuous buzzing. Gingerly he went to the next tree and climbed to the top.

It was the perfect observatory. From here, the whole forest spread out around Vasco like an endless green carpet. To the north, the harmony was broken by the apparition of sharp rocks delineating the new territory of mountains. Yet the buzzing grew louder. Vasco turned his head upstream of the river and noticed lots of expansive movement in the vegetation. Trees swung as if under a strange storm. Suddenly several of them fell, snapping as they disappeared in the sea of foliage.

Men are destroying the forest! was Vasco's immediate thought. *They're advancing toward us with their chain saws!*

He observed the progression of the work as trees were felled, exhaust fumes rose from the trucks, and saws buzzed. With a pang in his heart, Vasco knew that the tribe would not be able to linger in this territory they were starting to think of as home. It was too close to the river.

Vasco climbed down the tree, wondering how he was going to tell the others that they had to flee again. Would they listen to him? Would they place their trust in him once more?

He was deep in thought when he was startled by calls of distress. A few meters below, little Zeya was suspended from a dangling creeper, her body hanging in space. She had followed him!

11

Zeya

Vasco leaped with agility and landed just above Zeya, on a spot where the creeper still coiled around the branch. The blind female had knocked against it when she fell, and had had the reflex to close her claws around the rest of the dangling creeper.

"Don't move!" Vasco whispered. "I'll come and get you."

But in a glance he understood that if he came down to her, he wouldn't have enough strength to climb back up.

"Hurry!" Zeya begged. "I can't hold on any longer!"

Vasco had no choice. He leaned into the void and slid down the creeper until his paws came in contact with Zeya. Then he twisted his body so that Zeya could grab hold of his fur. Once her grip was firm, Vasco looked anxiously toward the trunk. He would have to gather momentum and swing. . . . Either luck would be on his side or they would both crash at the foot of the fig tree.

"Get ready," he said between clenched teeth.

"What are you doing?" Zeya demanded, sounding panicked. "You're scared. I can feel it."

"No, I'm not scared. Hang on to me as tight as you can!"

Vasco shifted his weight to one side of the creeper and then to the other in order to make it swing. Once he had gathered momentum, he propelled himself into the air. For a fraction of a second, he thought he was done for. But his snout banged against the trunk and he extended his paws to grip the bark. He slipped, but finally grabbed a twig farther down.

Zeya was shaking but stayed glued to him, her small claws digging into the flesh at his back and throat. Vasco held on to the twig and slowly hauled himself on top of it.

"Did you save us?" Zeya whispered as Vasco wedged himself in the nook of the tree, unable to move anymore.

"Yes. You can relax your grip. Your claws are killing me."

The little blind female loosened her grasp and dug her snout into Vasco's fur. He could feel her pulsing heart.

"How did you manage to come up here?" he asked, conscious of the effort Zeya had exerted to climb so high.

"I imitated you," she answered simply.

Imitated? Vasco looked at the little female in awe. He had never thought that a handicapped rat could accomplish such a task. Zeya's adaptive abilities were out of the ordinary.

"What do you see up there?" she asked with curiosity. "It must be very pleasant since you always go so high."

Vasco sighed. A shudder ran down his spine. He remembered the felled trees and the trucks advancing along the river. He had to warn the tribe that the refuge would soon no longer be safe.

"Climb on my back," he told Zeya with weariness. "And be sure to hold tight. I don't have the strength to come and save you a second time."

• • •

A while later, they were at the burrow. Joun and Nil seemed agitated. They ran in all directions, tearing moss from fallen branches, and hurried inside the nest with their harvest. Zeya steadily breathed in the air, then turned to Vasco.

"A female just gave birth," she announced.

Vasco also sniffed the air but did not detect any particular odor. The jungle exhaled its usual complex scents of dirt, mold, pepper, and sugar. He came near one of the entrances to the burrow, but Nil emerged and blocked his way.

"Itsa just gave birth to nine babies," she announced. "No male can come in."

Respectfully, Vasco stepped back and took a look at Zeya. She had truly smelled the newborns! This blind girl amazed him all the more.

"Nine new babies." He sighed. "It's really not a good time for this."

Vasco took a few leaps and stood atop a root to listen to the noises of the forest. Nothing could be heard but the cries of monkeys, the rustle of foliage, and the lapping of the river. But what about tomorrow?

Twilight was coming. Regus and Coben returned from their foraging expedition. At this time of day, they didn't stray far from the burrow—as darkness approached, the undergrowth became the dangerous territory of weasels and nocturnal birds. Vasco approached the beige rat to make him aware of his concern.

"We'll have to leave," he began.

Regus stopped. His whiskers were shining with sap, as if he had spent the day in a basket of fruit.

"Leave?" he said, sounding surprised. "Out of the question! We have everything we need right here."

"Men are coming," Vasco explained. "I saw their trucks by the shore of the river."

Coben sniffed Vasco with contempt. "You don't smell of slime, mud, or water. You're lying. You weren't anywhere near the river."

Vasco inhaled deeply to keep his calm. Men would not reach the site of their burrow so soon. Besides, Itsa and her nine babies could not possibly follow the tribe.

"Let's wait," Vasco said. "But be ready to flee again."

Regus sat back and started to lick his paws. "You should relax," he told Vasco. "Why don't you come hunt with me?"

Vasco observed the beige rat with care. In the past, they had been inseparable. They had roamed the city sewers together, and Regus had shown him the best waste bins. Sadness now invaded Vasco's heart. It was hard for him to admit, but since Regus had started sharing a nook in the burrow with Nil, he could hardly stand him. Jealousy separated them. So without a word of explanation, Vasco got up and moved off to return to his solitude.

As he passed behind the root of the fig tree, Zeya joined him.

"I'll follow you," she declared. "You saved my life today."

Vasco licked her head affectionately. Not long ago, he had saved Nil's life too, but it was as if she did not remember it. With bitterness, Vasco reflected that the memory of rats seemed as fleeting as clouds pushed along by the wind.

12

Still Farther Away from Men

A frightening crashing noise, followed by bird cries and the flapping of wings, awakened the tribe with a start. Vasco came out of a deep sleep and scurried outside. The catastrophe he feared was taking place.

"Men!" he shouted. "Men are coming."

Regus, Nil, and Joun emerged from the burrow. The chain saws had powered up. One of the large trees on the border of the river had just toppled not far from the rats' refuge, causing panic among the birds and monkeys. Soon the workers would reach the heart of the forest.

The wheels of the trucks would wreck the undergrowth, destroying all life in their path.

"Gather the females and little ones!" Regus commanded Joun. Then he turned to Vasco. "You were right," he admitted.

Soon all the rats assembled. Cries of anxiety rose from every corner. Where should they flee to? Some suggested returning to the town, but others refused since it meant crossing the cutting site and encountering the workers. Regus looked anxiously at Vasco.

"Let's head down the river," he suggested. "There must be villages downstream if the men float lumber that way."

Vasco swung his tail from side to side. He did not agree with Regus. Going back to humans seemed like a defeat. The tribe had not traveled from the big city to find itself in another one. They had to create a new way of life, far from humans.

"Why do you persist?" Regus asked him. "Maybe we weren't intended to live in the wild."

Vasco looked at the beige rat with contempt. "Are you afraid?"

"No," Regus answered, sounding offended. "But what if it's a mistake? What if the jungle doesn't want us?"

Attentive to the noise, Vasco grimaced. The machines were getting closer. The jungle was not rejecting the tribe, men were. He thought about the landscape he had seen atop the tree: the vast carpet of foliage, and to the north, the jagged rocks of the mountains. The machines would not be able to cross the mountain pass.

"We have to go north," Vasco said with confidence. "We must cross the pass and find refuge in a valley on the other side."

Regus listened to him calmly. "I hope you're right," he said finally.

Then he nodded and hurried toward the females and little ones who were emerging from the burrow. Vasco caught sight of Itsa, with a baby in her mouth, and remembered the nine newborns. It was going to be a long and dangerous journey for them. How would the tribe cope with nine helpless rats? Then Joun appeared with another baby in her mouth.

"We can't carry them all," Vasco told her. "The other females have enough of a burden with their own little ones."

Joun put the tiny baby down in front of her. Its hairless body, closed eyes, and pink nose made it look all the more helpless.

"I promised Itsa that the whole litter would be saved," she said. "The males have to carry the seven others."

"The males?" Vasco repeated, taken aback.

He took a look around. Regus, Coben, and the others were gathered near the roots of the fig tree, ready to go.

They had not wanted to dig the nest, so why would they ever agree to care for the babies like females?

At that moment, Nil came out of the refuge carrying another of the babies. She trotted up to Regus and deposited it between his paws. Vasco could hear the squeaks and groans of the males. But Nil persisted. She rubbed herself against Regus insistently, and circled around him while other females brought the remainder of the litter to the roots of the fig tree. They put the babies down as if they were offerings.

Suddenly another tree crashed by the river. All the rats curled up in terror. The buzzing of the machines drew nearer. It was time to go. Before Vasco's astounded eyes, Regus picked up the baby between his teeth and stood facing the males. Nil had convinced him.

The tribe left camp in a long and silent file. Regus and Vasco opened the way: the beige rat held the newborn in his jaws, and Vasco had Zeya on his back. Behind them Joun, Nil, and Itsa made sure that every baby was safe. Vasco was pleased that the males had shown a change in attitude. Even Coben, who was strong enough now, had been put in charge of one of the babies. He seemed vexed about his chore, but since Regus accepted the job, he did not dare refuse.

His snout to the ground, Vasco guided the tribe to the north. The jungle was strangely silent now. The trucks and chain saws had chased off all the animals, which was a great help to the rats. They could move forward without fearing encounters with enemies. But Vasco knew that this would not last once they were over the pass. New dangers would threaten them in the valley.

"Cheer up!" Zeya suddenly whispered in his ear. It was as if she could read his thoughts. "We'll make it."

After hours of walking in the undergrowth, Vasco realized that the ground was becoming steeper.

"Tell me what you feel, Zeya," he said, turning his head back to look at her.

"The air is getting heavier, and I hear insects. Night is not far."

Vasco looked up. The sky was hazy. The blind girl could perceive things so well but she could not see the breathtaking height of the pass they had to cross. Behind a mass of branches, the jagged rocks of the mountain rose, inaccessible and alarming.

Regus stopped near Vasco, out of breath. He put the baby down. The whole file of rats came to a halt. Again Zeya leaned in to Vasco's ear.

"I can hear a hollow sound, and I smell dampness," she said. "There must be a cave nearby."

Vasco put Zeya down and left to scout out the bushes. When he returned, he announced that he had found a rocky nook where the tribe would find shelter for the night.

13

The Cave

The long line of rats entered the cave as night was falling.

Without even consulting each other, Vasco and Regus hurried over to a rocky outcrop shaped like a giant basin. The slightly elevated spot would make an acceptable refuge and was out of reach for reptiles.

Joun started helping Itsa to settle in the sheltered spot. The young mother recovered her little ones and lay down on her side so that the babies could feed at her nipples.

Water oozed from everywhere in the cave. A thick

coat of moss covered the stalactites that hung from the ceiling. Vasco gathered the males around him and designated those who were still strong enough to forage for the group. Coben, impatient and irritated that he'd had to carry a baby all day, volunteered for the task.

"I'm a male," he said. "I'm supposed to go hunting, not be used as a mule!"

"We all have to help one another," Vasco answered. "Go hunting with Regus if you want, but tomorrow you still have to carry one of the newborns."

The young rat reared in defiance. "The babies slow us down! Without them we would already be over the pass!"

Vasco started circling Coben. He was angry. "Tomorrow we'll go over the pass with the nine babies, whether you like it or not. If you refuse to help the tribe, you can leave and live your life alone."

Then, nose to nose with Regus, he added aggressively, "Since you were so proud of living a solitary life, no doubt you'll teach Coben since he listens only to you!"

Regus arched his back and groaned, as if to say, *Why are you taking it out on me?* Vasco paused for a second, regretting his outburst. Yes, Regus was solitary. But for a long time now he had lived by the rules of the tribe. The proof was that he had followed them this far, in spite of his doubts and reluctance.

At that moment, Nil appeared out of the darkness and came between the two rats. She looked tired but stood her ground.

"The females are hungry," she said, to cut the dispute short.

Regus spat and gave the signal to go. Without a glance at Vasco, he trotted to the exit, followed by the other males.

Nil fell back heavily on all fours and gave Vasco's flank a little blow with her snout. It was clear that Nil did not want him to challenge Regus. Then she moved off to be near Joun.

A little puzzled, Vasco remained by himself a long while. The tribe had obeyed him today, but he knew that he no longer had Regus' confidence. In fact, he realized that they did not share the same dream. Vasco wanted to establish a tribe with a different way of life—one without confrontation or warfare, one that was in harmony with the rest of the world. Regus, on the other hand, had always accepted violence as a natural way of life. What Vasco aspired to was simpler: he wanted to find a good hunting ground, and to eat freely while defending his territory.

Aware of his differences with Regus, Vasco started turning in circles, feeling deeply sad and terribly lonesome.

"I can hear something," Zeya said, suddenly coming close to him. "From the back of the cave."

"Leave me alone," Vasco said. "You bother me with your omens."

Zeya stayed silent but did not go away. "You're sad because Nil is expecting?" she said finally.

Vasco turned around as if electrified. "Nil is expecting?" he repeated, incredulous.

Zeya brushed him with the tips of her whiskers. She knew everything, she guessed everything. Vasco should have known. That was the reason Regus had agreed to carry the baby that morning. Nil had made him understand that he had to because he would soon have little ones of his own to protect. It was also the reason why Vasco felt such distance between them.

"So? Do you hear it?" Zeya insisted. "There's something moving at the back of the cave."

Vasco heard nothing. His ears, nostrils, and whiskers were of no use anymore. Jealousy swept away every other sensation. He wanted to rush out of the cave, to run after Regus and fight him.

But as he was about to rush outside, he picked up the sounds that worried Zeya. The unfamiliar noise was getting closer.

"Let's find shelter!" Zeya begged. "I'm scared."

Vasco's blood froze in his veins. He grabbed Zeya with

his teeth and ran to the basin where the females were gathered. He found them crouched against the ground, their ears attuned to the strange sound.

"What is it?" Nil murmured.

"I don't know. Hide under the stones!"

In a second, the tribe dispersed amid lots of squeaking. Vasco pushed Zeya against Nil in a nook. Now the noise was a full-blown din that sounded like the rustle of fabric mixed with high-pitched animal sounds.

"Take shelter!" Nil begged Vasco when she noticed that he was still exposed.

"No," he said.

He stood on his hind legs and waited for the arrival of the enemy. He did not care about danger anymore. He needed to fight. Whatever this approaching beast turned out to be, he would confront it—even if it cost him his life.

As he tensed himself, ready to leap, Vasco felt a draft. The noise grew deafening. He looked up. Dark and shapeless things flew above him, followed by others that barely grazed him.

Then, as suddenly as it came, the noise moved toward the exit of the cave. Vasco rushed behind it in time to see hundreds of winged shapes making their way into the nighttime sky.

"Flying mice," he whispered, flabbergasted.

He came down on all fours, exhausted, his muscles stiff with cramps, his body as cold as ice. Zeya and Nil rushed over to him. Their presence warmed him up and he started breathing normally. The bats had disappeared and silence had returned.

When Zeya licked his whiskers, Vasco realized that he was happy to be alive after all.

14

A Quiet Valley

At daybreak, the tribe left the cave and started climbing toward the pass. This time the males took charge of the babies without complaining. Regus and Vasco led the way out in front, as they had the day before.

The higher they climbed, the sparser the vegetation. The large trees were replaced by smaller ones, and the ferns were gradually replaced with thorny bushes. From time to time, brightly colored flowers emerged from the bramble.

At the back of the file, Itsa and Nil were lagging.

Vasco turned to keep an eye on them and adjusted his rhythm to give them time to catch up. Now that he knew Nil was pregnant, he worried that maybe she wouldn't be able to keep pace.

Higher up, clouds of fog delayed their progress. Vasco and Regus took frequent pauses to make sure that no one was lost, then started up again. At times, they heard cries in the sky, probably birds of prey. But the mantle of fog that covered the mountain offered them protection, so they kept going. Even as hunger and thirst started to torture them, they plodded on. Nil and Itsa were unlikely to start again if the rhythm was broken.

Later in the day, Vasco noticed that the slope of the ground had reversed. Under his paws, little pebbles loosened and skittered down along a steep slope.

"The pass," he whispered. "We've crossed it."

Suddenly the fog lifted above them, and the sun inundated the ridge of the surrounding mountains. Vasco contemplated the imposing and wild landscape of dark canyons, forests, and, lower down, streams running into one another to fall in cascades on the ferns of the valley. It looked as if no human had ever set foot in this kingdom of greenery and rocks.

As the tribe gathered around him, a piercing cry ripped the silence. They were all startled.

"A bird of prey," Regus said.

"It's much bigger than an owl!" Coben said, letting go of the little one he was carrying.

The rapacious bird spun in the blue sky, right above their heads. It couldn't miss them. Vasco was choked by his heartbeats.

"Run!" he yelled. "Straight ahead!"

While the males darted down the slope, Vasco looked behind him for Nil. He leaped toward her, but at the same moment he caught sight of Zeya's little pink snout searching her way through the crowd. Vasco grabbed her by the skin of her back and glanced at Nil with regret.

"Go!" said the young rat. "Regus will look after me."

The cry of the eagle grew more shrill. Without losing a moment, Vasco fled down the rocky slope. He hurtled along the side of the mountain. In front of him he saw the tails and paws of his companions, who were running and taking cover under stones, dry bramble, or any other hiding spot that presented itself. Vasco leaped, slipped, and rolled on his side, all the while holding Zeya, who was making herself as small as possible. When he regained his balance, Vasco realized that he had slipped several meters. His fall had been stopped by some bushes. He raised his snout and watched as the eagle suddenly dove to the ground higher up on the pass.

"No!" A terrible anguish tightened Vasco's heart. The eagle had grabbed a victim and was flying away swiftly toward the mountain peak. Vasco looked at the small shape held tight in its claws, the lifeless body of . . .

"Nil!" he cried out.

Only the silence of the mountains, the sun, the bush, and the hard ground were left.

Vasco was desperate. Nil . . . Nil had been taken away! Vasco lay on the ground and stayed there as if he too were dead.

Later, he heard noises around him: the sound of paws on the stones, accompanied by panting. Zeya nibbled at his ear.

"Get up," she said.

But Vasco could not get up. He was drained of energy. What was the use of going down to the valley now? Why keep on traveling? Why flee danger when more danger always lay in wait? The tranquility that he was looking for did not exist. He might as well stay here.

"Get up," Zeya insisted. "I need you to guide me."

Suddenly Nil's scent reached his nostrils. But he still did not move, sure that it was a dream.

"Is Vasco hurt?" It was Nil's voice.

"No," Zeya answered. "He was waiting for you."

Vasco lifted his head. Nil and Regus were here, in front of him, their fur covered in dirt.

"The eagle grabbed one of Itsa's babies," Regus explained. "Let's leave the mountain before it comes back."

Quickly Vasco stood up. Nil was alive! She scurried

toward the valley with Regus, while the other rats of the tribe came out of their hiding spots and gathered to follow them.

"So are you coming?" Zeya asked, raising her pink snout toward Vasco.

• • •

A multitude of torrents ran across the valley, forming small lakes of clear water tinted with a shade of ochre. Gigantic tualang trees, also known as honeybee trees, raised their silvery trunks among mango and monkeybread trees, also known as baobabs. After the rocky terrain of the mountains, the rats now found their paws on a thick, spongy layer of dead leaves and heather, which formed a pleasant carpet. As the day ended, monkeys called languorously, and swarms of bees buzzed furiously around the branches of the tualangs, a noise that reminded the tribe of the chain saws. But Vasco knew that the lumberjacks would not come here. *We've come east at last,* he thought. *Olmo was right.* He let out a long cry to thank the old rat from the freighter. The tribe could stop now and dig a new burrow, close to the water.

Exhausted, Itsa retrieved her litter and lay on the moss to feed them. Joun and the other females went to the brook, leaving the males to forage for food. As he looked at Nil, Vasco realized that she would give birth in this quiet and remote place. A feeling of plenitude came over him. The rats' long journey seemed to have ended at last.

Regus organized the hunt, while Vasco explored the surroundings. Various smells of moss, flowers, and rotten fruit excited his nostrils. But as he went farther away from the water, he detected a scent stronger than the others. An animal had urinated recently on this spot. He looked up and saw something move in the leaves of a small palm tree. Softly he approached the tree. The smell intensified. It seemed to be that of a rodent but was not totally identifiable. Vasco stopped, stood on his hind legs, and pricked his ears. A noise led him to believe that the animal had seen him and decided to run away. He shuddered. This heavenly spot might not be as quiet as he had thought.

15

The Snake Hunter

Over the following days, in spite of Vasco's warnings, carelessness spread in the tribe. The females were now adept enough to rapidly dig a large and solid burrow not far from the brook, while the young ones played, squabbled, and fought nearby. Itza's young ones were getting stronger. They wandered out of the nest without supervision.

"Nil is nervous," Joun announced one morning. "She's going to give birth soon."

Vasco's heart started to race. His eyes looked for

Regus but the beige rat was not to be found. Since they had settled here, he spent most of his time far from the burrow, hunting with Coben. Sometimes they brought back fruit whose pulp was red and creamy, sometimes caterpillar larvae, even bird eggs fallen from nests. Thanks to them the tribe was well provided for, but Vasco could feel how worried Nil was each time Regus went off.

"I'll go get Regus," he said to Joun.

Zeya appeared. "I'm coming with you!" she declared.

He did not try to dissuade her. The young blind rat was now always by his side, as faithful as his shadow. She followed him everywhere, guessed and imitated each of his movements, and displayed such ease in the trees that Vasco almost forgot that she could not see.

They started running toward the silvery trunk of the honeybee tree. Regus' hunting territory started just beyond there.

They had hardly reached the giant tree when they heard frightened squeaks. Zeya raised her snout.

"The smell of blood," she whispered.

Two males suddenly sprang out of a bush. In their panic, they got tangled up in knotty twigs. Vasco rushed over to them.

"A snake!" shouted the first one. "Regus tried to steal its eggs!"

"He's still over there with Coben!" added the second rat as he fled to the burrow.

His body shaking, Vasco turned to Zeya. "I forbid you to follow me! Go back to the nest!"

His voice was so commanding that the blind female did not protest but turned around and started back, guided by the scent left by the two frightened males. As Vasco wormed his way under the bush he pricked up his ears, but except for the irritating gurgling of the langur monkeys who lived in the canopy of branches, he did not hear a thing.

He was about to climb onto a tree trunk to get his bearings when he heard the noise of a fight at ground level. The hissing of rats . . . and of a snake! Suddenly Coben appeared on top of a mossy rock. He was out of breath, and leaves stuck to his fur as if he had rolled on the ground. Vasco rushed in his direction. Where was Regus?

As he saw Vasco approach, Coben let out a little cry of victory and looked behind him. At the bottom of the rock, Vasco discovered Regus, his teeth planted in the head of a long grayish snake. The reptile contorted itself, his tail whipping the air, but Regus held tight. After a few jerks, the enemy was vanquished.

"He got it!" Coben said, jumping down from the rock. "We only wanted its eggs, but we got even more!"

Regus lifted his trophy in his mouth and carried the body to the burrow. Vasco watched him, flabbergasted. He had never seen a rat attack a snake of that size and win the fight.

He joined Regus and Coben as they made a triumphant entrance in the burrow. Vasco tried to contain a wave of anger. Nil was about to give birth and Regus had blithely attacked a formidable enemy, placing his life and those of others in danger. What was he thinking? Food was plentiful in the jungle. He did not have to engage a snake.

The two males who had fled the fight had passed word of Regus' battle; the females and young rats had gathered near the river, waiting in anguish to know if Regus was dead. When they saw him approach with the snake in his mouth, a concert of admiring squeaks burst forth.

Vasco looked at Joun, who rushed inside the nest to inform Nil that her companion was safe and sound.

"You should have been there!" Coben told the group. "Regus overcame the snake in three bites!"

The beige rat nonchalantly threw the corpse toward the females and older males who did not hunt. Then he sat down and started to lick his flanks to get rid of twigs and leaves. Vasco came close to him.

"Do you want to congratulate me?" Regus asked, looking up.

"What you did deserves only contempt," Vasco said. "Nil is about to give birth. You should be with her!"

"Why?" Regus went on, surprised. "She can manage by herself."

Vasco ground his teeth. The fur on his back stood on end. He knew deep down that Regus was only guided by his hunter instinct. No male was ever interested in his offspring. Yet he was expecting a different behavior from the beige rat.

"You could have been killed!" Vasco continued. "And the snake would have disposed of Coben in no time!"

Regus stopped grooming and turned to Vasco. Calmly he pointed out that nothing had happened.

"Look at them!" Regus said, pointing to the rats who were digging their teeth deep into the snake's body. "They have a treat." Then he looked squarely at Vasco and added, "You've never been a good hunter. So let me do my duty for the tribe and you go back to playing in the trees with your little blind female. I'll be the better for it."

Vasco was filled with rage. Without warning, he leaped on his former friend and bit down cruelly into his side. Regus shouted out in pain but managed to roll away and stand on his paws.

Around them, everyone stood still. Females stopped eating, young ones were hushed, males froze in anticipation.

It seemed as if even the wind had stopped playing with the foliage.

Regus was slightly wounded and breathed heavily. Only his nostrils moved, but Vasco knew that he was ready to fight back. So Vasco curled up and started to click his teeth, an indication that he would not submit to Regus.

At that moment, Joun ran out of the burrow.

"There are six! Nil just gave birth to six little ones!" she shouted loudly.

16

Apart

Vasco turned his head and hesitated for a second. That was all Regus was waiting for. Without looking at Joun, he threw himself at Vasco and dug his claws into his rival's flanks. Then he jumped out of Vasco's reach.

An awful burning sensation took Vasco's breath away. The pain was so acute that his vision blurred. Colors mixed together while vague shapes moved around him and squeaks of protest reached his ears. Then he felt a tepid fluid run along his fur. He fell on his side.

When he came back to his senses, Joun and the other

females surrounded him, forming a barrier between him and Regus. A dismayed silence fell on the group. How could such a fight erupt? Vasco and Regus were the two leaders of the tribe—it seemed senseless.

"Vasco was in the wrong!" Coben exclaimed suddenly. "He attacked Regus without provocation!"

A hostile murmur spread among the group, turning Vasco's heart icy. When he managed to get up, his gaze met Joun's hard stare. He expected to hear the worst possible blame from her, but the old female only eyed him up and down silently.

"Vasco was in the wrong!" repeated the others. "He's no longer worthy of our trust!"

Vasco began to shiver. His authority, already weakened, was now entirely put in question.

Suddenly Joun stepped away from the group. "Where is Zeya?" she asked, worried. She looked at Vasco. "You were supposed to look after her and I don't see her anywhere!"

Vasco felt he had received a second blow to his flanks. *Zeya!* How could he have forgotten her? Before rushing to Regus' aid, he had told her to return to the burrow. She should be here. But Joun shook her head: the blind female had not come back.

Anguish replaced humiliation. Vasco broke through the circle of females surrounding him, looked at the males gathered around Regus, then ran toward the tualang tree where he had left Zeya.

At the bottom of the tree, he sniffed the ground. He lifted dead leaves with the tip of his snout, sniffed the bushes, upturned stones, retraced his steps. . . . He was about to give up when he finally caught the scent of the blind rat on the bark of the honeybee tree, a few centimeters off the ground. Of course! Zeya had managed to climb!

Vasco gathered his courage and shot up the trunk. His wound was painful, but he planted his claws in the bark, arched his back, and pulled himself up to the first branches.

"Zeya!" he called.

Nothing. There was no sound other than the buzzing of bees. He moved higher, searching for the scent of the young rat, and ended up at the top of the tree. Under the scorching midday sun, the monkeys had retreated into the shade, leaving the top to insects and birds.

Vasco followed Zeya's scent along a horizontal branch. He wondered why she had gone so high when she was supposed to hurry back to the burrow. What had happened?

But Vasco shuddered when the branch started to bend. He was at the very tip of it, where it divided into leafy little twigs. Zeya's scent had vanished. He looked down. The branches of a neighboring tree spread below him. What if Zeya had fallen?

A feeling of weariness came over Vasco. If Zeya had plummeted, if she was dead . . . then there was nothing else to lose. He might as well take his chances.

Without hesitation, he jumped from the branch. Leaves whipped his snout as he stretched his paws in front of him and landed on the neighboring tree. He moved forward and again found the scent of the blind rat. She had taken a dangerous route from tree to tree, like the flying squirrels that Vasco had described to her when they lived in the burrow next to the river.

He continued his search, climbing up, climbing down, jumping from branch to branch. As he was about to leap into the air again, his eyes were attracted by a dark spot on the ground. He leaned forward. The motionless body of a rat lay at the bottom of the tree.

In a few leaps, Vasco was by the small corpse.

It was not Zeya.

He turned the body around and sniffed it. He recognized Faer, one of the males of the tribe. Lifting the head of the dead rat, he discovered an ugly wound on his left eye, as well as traces of deep bites on his chest.

All his senses on alert, Vasco explored the surroundings. He stopped suddenly when he picked up Zeya's scent. Then a noise startled him. He did not even have time to turn around when the blind female ran out of a bush.

"Vasco! I was so scared," she said, trotting up to him and rubbing herself against his wounded side. "Are you bleeding?" she asked, sounding alarmed. "Did they attack you too?"

"Who?" Vasco inquired.

"Those who killed Faer and Sosk."

Vasco stepped back. He did not understand. He had seen Faer's body, but where was Sosk?

Zeya pointed to a bush. "Over there, at the back. He's dead."

Unable to move, Vasco tried to gather his thoughts.

"I picked up their scent when you left me near the tualang," Zeya explained. "It was a recent scent, so I followed it here." She raised her pink snout to Vasco. "Those who killed Faer and Sosk are rats like us," she said gravely. "But they're a native species."

"How can you be so sure?"

"When I came near Sosk, they were still here. They saw me. I thought they were going to kill me as well, but one of them noticed that I was blind. It was their chief. He ordered them to spare me. Then they left, but I had time to smell them. They were rats. Nomads, probably, because their fur smelled of salt and marsh. There's no salty water around here."

Vasco's head spun. Wild rats . . . nomads . . . surely much bigger than those of his tribe, much stronger, better adapted to life in the jungle. It was their smell that he had noticed near the water the day they arrived. And the movements in the palm tree leaves had to have been one of the nomad rats spying on him.

"Come!" he told Zeya. "We have to warn the others."

17

War or Peace?

On his way back to the burrow, Vasco realized that if he wanted to be heard, he had to keep a low profile and apologize to Regus, whatever the cost. So when he saw the beige rat at the entrance to the nest, he pushed aside his pride and flattened himself submissively. Coben and the other males were suspicious of his behavior.

In the silence that followed, Vasco swallowed with difficulty. The scene reminded him of when he had crawled in front of Akar, begging for the rat's protection in spite of his repulsion for him. His snout in the moss, it took great effort for him to beg for Regus' pardon. Regus hesitated to answer, so Vasco slowly got up and addressed the whole tribe.

"I led you up to this place hoping to find a permanent refuge in this part of the jungle," he said. "Regus made me aware of his doubts but I did not want to listen to him. Now I understand that I made a mistake. Peace is nowhere to be found."

He stopped. The females and young ones listened to him without understanding what he meant. Vasco then turned and looked for Zeya. She was standing a few steps away from him, her ears pricked.

"Zeya!" Vasco called. "Tell them what you discovered!"

Timidly the blind female came forward; it would be the first time she addressed the tribe. She told them about the bodies of Faer and Sosk, and of her encounter with the nomad rats, and the fact that their chief had spared her life.

A muted murmur ran through the assembly. Some started to call the names of the two missing rats as if to make sure that they were not hidden near the burrow; others cried and lamented as the females called the little ones who had strayed away from them. Now Regus faced Vasco, putting an end to the brouhaha.

"Are you sure of what you and Zeya are saying?" he asked.

"I saw Faer, lying down and lifeless. He had deep wounds."

"But you did not see his assailants," Regus pointed out. "Why should we trust a blind female?"

"It is true that Zeya does not have use of her eyes," Vasco acknowledged, lowering his head. "But her ears and sense of smell are more acute than any of ours. She can be trusted."

Regus came down on all fours. He remembered that he had sent Faer and Sosk to hunt beyond their usual territory. They had probably entered that of the nomad rats, which had caused their demise. If they were dead, it was mostly his fault.

At that moment, Coben stepped out of the ranks and let out an outraged cry. He wanted to mobilize his companions and lead them to the camp of these new foes to destroy them.

"If they are rats, we can confront them!" he spat out. "We have to fight back!"

Immediately the other rats clamored for vengeance: Faer and Sosk had been strong hunters, and those who had killed them deserved punishment for their crime. Worked up, Coben arched his back and exposed his teeth, offering to lead the punitive expedition. But to Vasco's relief, Regus did not seem to agree. He came near Coben.

"No one appointed you chief," he told him. "Until otherwise decided, Vasco is the one in charge of our tribe."

"Vasco?" Coben choked. "But he wounded you! He doesn't know what he's doing! You said so yourself: he's not even a good hunter! The best he can do is take care of a blind female!"

Regus hesitated and gazed at each member of the tribe. Vasco watched him, in the silence remembering how Regus had always wanted to live his life without submitting to the rules of a group. Then he remembered the strange moment on the freighter when he and Vasco had been alone at the top of the exhaust stack. Ourga and Akar had just died; the wind and the sea had been unleashing their ire around them. It was then that Regus had acknowledged Vasco as leader.

Now Regus turned toward Vasco and with the tip of his snout forced him to look up.

"What is your decision?" Regus asked him.

Vasco moved back slightly. Though Regus was deferring to him, Vasco no longer believed that he was able to make decisions. Regus was in a better position to do that. He was strong, courageous, determined . . . and he had a family now, six little ones and a female to back him up. Vasco told him as much.

"You are right, but I do not have any claims to the

tribe," Regus declared. "I just followed you, hunting and fighting enemies along the way. I don't have your wisdom, Vasco. If we are still alive, it is thanks to you."

Joun had kept silent until now, but she approached Vasco. She seemed so tired and old.

"I agree with Regus," she declared. "In spite of what you did earlier, you are the only one here who knows what is best for us."

Vasco moved farther back, then cast a glance at Coben. The young rat was outraged but silent. He was too respectful of Regus to try to oppose him.

"What do you decide?" Regus repeated, pressing him.

"We must wait," Vasco finally whispered. "If violence is the answer to violence, then the future of the tribe is quite somber. Let's stay vigilant. We will not wander on the nomad rats' territory. They spared Zeya, which is a good sign. If we do not challenge them, we may be able to get along with them."

When he heard these words, Coben scurried off. Drool hung from his mouth, and his eyes were full of revolt.

"The tribe needs a real leader," he cried, looking back. "Not a coward!"

He had hardly left the burrow when Regus ordered two other males to follow and keep him in check.

"Your decision is the right one," Regus added, looking

at Vasco. "Nil will be pleased to know that we are not go-ing to war."

Vasco nodded, then sighed as Regus left to go to his nest. Underground, in one of the nooks of the burrow, Nil was waiting with her little ones. Regus had once again refused all responsibility and returned to rest near his family.

Vasco was left alone.

18

Courage and Wisdom

Night was falling over the jungle.

The rats were used to the afternoon song of the gibbons and the furious cackles of the macaques in the last rays of sunlight. At this time of day the whole tribe took shelter in the burrow, for it was then that large mammals—bearded boars, tapirs, and otters—took possession of the area.

But tonight, in spite of the danger, Vasco stood at the entrance to the nest. His ears twitched in all directions and anxiety made his nostrils quiver. In the oppressive and humid atmosphere, swarms of insects twirled around, while birds flew from the tops of trees, squawking, over the brook. Coben and the two other males were not back yet.

"Something has happened," Vasco said to Zeya, who as usual had nestled against him.

At that moment, Regus appeared in the corridor that led to the exit. They exchanged a worried glance, then Regus joined Vasco outside. His fur exhaled a smell of sour milk and warm moss, the imprint left by Nil's little ones.

"We can't do anything tonight." Regus sighed. "Come inside the shelter."

Vasco's heart tightened. Regus was right. The dark coat of night was covering the forest. It was too dangerous to stray off. But if Coben had dragged the other two into the nomad rats' camp, the situation was sure to escalate.

Vasco was about to head back underground when he heard distant cries. Right away, Zeya raised her snout and sniffed in the direction of the wind.

"It's Coben!" she announced.

As the cries drew nearer, Vasco and Regus tensed up, ready to leap at whatever danger confronted them. But Zeya was right. It was Coben who appeared suddenly from the bushes and ran toward the entrance of the nest.

Out of breath, his fur ruffled and dirty, he looked as if he were coming out of a mud bath. He had fought—that much was clear. Vasco started shaking while Regus groaned and bared his teeth.

"They killed two more of ours!" Coben explained. "I had a narrow escape. But it was war!"

"What happened?" Regus inquired tightly.

Coben lowered his head and said nothing. Vasco drew near him. It was obvious that in spite of the warnings, Coben had gone to the nomad rats' camp and provoked them.

"I just wanted to see Sosk and Faer with my own eyes," Coben explained. "I wasn't looking for a fight!"

He recounted how the two young rats who followed him had tried to keep him from going where he wanted. As they blocked his way, Coben pushed and shoved them. Their quarrel attracted the attention of the nomad rats. Without even a warning, the nomads fell from the trees and attacked them.

"There were four against me," added Coben. "I fought well. When I fled, only two of them were left!"

Vasco felt completely discouraged. Coben did not realize the consequence of his mistake. The nomads would now want to avenge the deaths of their own. They would detect Coben's scent and follow the trail up to the refuge.

"They didn't pursue me," Coben assured them. "I ran fast!"

"Maybe," Regus said gravely. "But they'll surely attack at dawn. We have to get ready to be ahead of them."

He disappeared inside the burrow, Coben on his heels, to explain the situation to the rest of the tribe.

Vasco remained with Zeya, amid the worrisome shadows and scents of the night. He knew that he would not be able to prevent Regus from fighting the nomad rats. This new incident tilted the balance to the side of force. And yet Vasco was certain that it was possible to act otherwise—to negotiate, talk, find a compromise so that both tribes agreed to share the territory and avoid a massacre. But if he mentioned this to the others, they would accuse him of being a traitor and chase him from the tribe. He had to act alone.

"I'm here too," Zeya pointed out, as if reading his thoughts again.

Vasco turned to her. Her courage and wisdom continued to astonish him.

"You will come with me," he told her. "We will leave at daybreak and find the nomads' chief. We have to act quickly, before Regus gives the signal to attack. You will walk in front and guide me."

He thought some more and rubbed his snout against Zeya's head. "If their chief spared you once, he will spare you again. At least, that's what I hope!"

19

An Unexpected Attack

Daylight was just breaking beyond the tall trees when Vasco and Zeya began to climb up the honeybee tree. Every rat was still asleep when they left the nest, including Regus and Coben, who were so overcome by fatigue that they had collapsed at the entrance of the main corridor.

In the early morning mist, droplets of dew covered leaves and moss. The trunk of the tree was more slippery than it was later in the day, which made the climb more difficult. Yet Vasco and Zeya had acquired such agility that they reached the high branches with relative ease.

Zeya led the way with assurance. Darkness was no handicap for her since she lived in perpetual night. Vasco, on the other hand, was more hesitant. When he reached the tip of the first branch, fear paralyzed him.

"Jump!" Zeya encouraged him from the neighboring tree. "Follow my voice!"

She kept sending short squeaks to make it easier for him. Holding his breath, Vasco jumped, went through the foliage, hung on a branch a few centimeters lower, and crouched near Zeya long enough to catch his breath.

They were over the first obstacle, but many more remained before they reached the nomads' camp. Vasco hoped that Regus would not attempt something foolish before then.

• • •

The first one to open his eyes was Coben. He jumped immediately onto his paws and pushed his snout into Regus' coat. Dawn was approaching. It was time to gather the troops.

The beige rat shook himself. In the silent burrow, he looked for Nil and the little ones, who were still sleeping huddled against their mother. He watched them a moment in silence, experiencing for the first time a feeling of fear. For nothing in the world would he put the lives of these fragile babies in danger. The battle had to take place as far as possible from the burrow.

Joun came over to Regus from a nearby nook and looked at him anxiously. Was he sure that this attack was the right solution? she asked. Had he spoken to Vasco about it?

"There is nothing more to decide," Regus answered firmly. "Coben killed two of their own. If we want to live here, we have to fight our enemies to gain the right to stay."

A shadow passed across the tired eyes of the old rat. Regus knew she had known many fights, many defeats, many deaths, as well as fratricidal hatred. And he knew her strength had been dwindling lately.

"What good is it to fight if it's always to lose the ones you love?" she whispered.

Regus sensed the presence of Lek near her. He could see him, standing on his hind legs, and the next second, killed by Ourga's bite. But Regus could not back down now. The tribe had no choice. Vasco himself had admitted that the tranquility he was looking for did not exist anywhere.

He rubbed his snout against Joun's to console her, although he knew that it was in vain.

"I leave Nil and my little ones in your care," he added before leaving the burrow.

• • •

"There we are!" Zeya whispered as she stopped at the tip of a dead twig that had fallen across the bushes. "I smell the scent of marsh and salt."

Behind her, Vasco stood still, his snout in the air. The wind was carrying the strange smell attached to the nomad rats. They didn't hear anything for the moment. Above them the sky was now so pale it seemed transparent. Clouds of fog still hung on the tops of the mountains at the border of the valley. In a moment, the first shouts of the monkeys would ring in the forest. Vasco shuddered.

"I will close my eyes," he said, "and you will be my guide as if I too were blind. If they discover that I am fit, they won't even listen to a word I say."

Zeya sighed.

"Are you scared?" Vasco asked her.

"Yes."

He gave her a little stroke with his snout to reassure her. "Let's go."

• • •

"Wait!" Regus ordered as he stopped at the edge of the brook.

All the males were gathered behind him, their backs arched, ready to fight. Coben was already clicking his teeth to impress enemies still out of sight.

Regus lowered his head and began to sniff at the banks. His sense of smell did not betray him. Alien rats had left their marks: droppings and prints on the ground, as well as on the weeds.

He raised his snout. "They're here, very close by," he whispered.

A tense silence fell on the group. Like antennas, the ears of the rats picked up the surrounding noises of gurgling water, droplets of dew gliding over the leaves, the buzzing of insects. . . . The whole jungle seemed on the lookout, awaiting an event that might disrupt everything.

Coben jerked and turned around. "There!"

Suddenly, in an unfurling of cries and wild squeaks, dozens of huge rats surged from the bushes. Regus stood up as tall as he could among his group. The nomad rats had been quicker! In the blink of an eye, they cornered Regus and his companions. Impressively strong muscles appeared through their short and clear fur, and their sharp teeth were visible in their snarling mouths.

A shudder of terror ran along Regus' spine. The fight would take place here, only a few meters away from the entrance of the burrow . . . close to Nil and his little ones.

20

Two Blind Rats

The refuge of the nomad rats was dug at the bottom of a huge mossy rock, sheltered by dwarf palm trees and heather. When they saw Zeya and Vasco approach their nest, two young rats sounded the alert with surprisingly hoarse squeaks. They rushed back to the rock, while Vasco and Zeya came to a standstill, trying to remain composed. The slightest sign of nervousness would derail their plan.

Soon some females rushed out of the hole and stood as a barrier against the intruders. They all started to squeak at the same time, but since Vasco and Zeya did not show signs of moving away, they hushed up, silently taking the measure of the two strangers.

Zeya moved toward them and lowered her snout to the ground to indicate that their intentions were peaceful. Vasco fought his desire to open his eyes. For now, he would have to rely on his sense of hearing and his sense of smell. He could hear the grinding of teeth and the murmur of questioning whispers. In turn, he crouched in front of the females.

"We do not want to hurt you," he spoke up. "Zeya and I are blind. We have come to meet the chief of your tribe."

The females seemed unconvinced. Vasco gave a start when he heard one of them whip the air with her tail. He was about to speak again when a noise made him jerk his head. A male had jumped down to the bottom of the rock, and his musky scent invaded Vasco's nostrils.

"I recognize the little female!" announced the newcomer. "It is true that she is blind. I spared her life when she was nosing around here."

The females chirped and walked back a few steps, tightly pressed together. But, gradually, the presence of the male seemed to calm them down. Vasco turned his head toward him, keeping his eyes closed.

"Are you the chief of the tribe?" he asked.

The big rat remained silent. Vasco could hear him

sniffing as he circled them. He was probably nosing out the smells of humans, of garbage cans, of the town, and of the harbor, which were steeped in Vasco's coat.

"You belong to the tribe that set up quarters near the brook," the rat said finally. "One of yours killed two of my hunters last night."

Vasco took a deep breath. "It was a young one," he pleaded. "He got scared and defended himself. But we are only looking for peace." He repeated his question: "Are you the chief of this tribe?"

One of the females moved forward. Vasco guessed this from the snapping of twigs.

"Kuok is indeed our chief," she said. "What do you want?"

Vasco had a renewed surge of confidence. The strange delegation that he formed with Zeya seemed to disarm the nomad rats. Everything was going as he desired: they were protected by their handicap. He got up and nodded gently before speaking to the assembly. He told them how his tribe had fled the town to escape humans, and how they had crossed the ocean. He told them of their arrival at the harbor, of their journey on the roof of the train, then of their discovery of the shantytown, and finally of their decision to move to the jungle to escape men.

Kuok and the females listened attentively. No sign of aggression disrupted Vasco's story.

"All we want is to live peacefully on this land," he concluded. "The jungle is immense and food plentiful. Nothing prevents us from cohabitating."

Kuok groaned. "The young male who killed two of my hunters did not seem to share your views."

"Coben is impulsive," Vasco assured him as he resumed his submissive posture. "He acted alone and against orders."

Kuok pondered this. The speech of this blind rat pleased him. Vasco's tribe had crossed the world seeking a refuge, so in a way they were also nomads.

He approached Vasco and asked him to raise his head.

"Your courage and wisdom are an honor to your people," he said. "But for the peace . . . it is too late."

Vasco's heart sank. He suddenly realized that he had missed an important detail: apart from Kuok, no other male was present. Where were they?

"My hunters have already gone to your burrow," Kuok confessed. "They want to avenge our slain brothers, and I'm afraid they will show no mercy."

Vasco cried in despair. As he and Zeya had been making their way from tree to tree, the attack on his tribe was unfolding on the ground! As he had been pleading with Kuok, the fight was in full swing near the burrow.

He turned to Kuok. "They must be stopped! The massacre must be stopped!"

Kuok hesitated. It was clear that he had never met a rat like Vasco. Usually each tribe went its own way without paying attention to others. Vasco knew that Kuok must be wondering if this was a trap.

"I could try to stop the fight," he said at last. "But what proof of your good faith can you give me?"

Vasco pondered. Kuok was right to have doubts. What proof could he give him? Worried, Zeya approached Vasco and buried her snout in his fur. Suddenly Vasco had the answer.

"The proof of my sincerity," he began, "is to confess that I lied to you." He opened his eyes. "Zeya is blind, but I am not."

Right away Kuok and the females leaped toward him, their backs arched and their voices squeaking.

Vasco tried to quell his fear. "Listen to me, Kuok!" he begged. "I lied to you but all I wanted was to reach you without being slaughtered. Now I am at your mercy. Keep me prisoner if you want, but order your troops to spare my tribe."

When he dared to look up again, Vasco laid eyes upon Kuok, whose impressive muscles were those of a strong climber. The powerful chief of the nomads could kill him with a single blow of his paw.

Yet the look he gave Vasco was strangely calm. And by his side a female with a golden coat watched him with curiosity.

"This rat is telling the truth," she said softly. "If not, why would he put his life in our hands?"

Kuok looked at her, then at Vasco. "I rely on Tulai's judgment. Leave the blind female here as a hostage and come with me. We will stop the fight."

21

Too Late?

Near the brook, the situation was desperate. Seeing that several of the males had been bitten to death, Regus wanted to move the fight to the undergrowth. He gave the signal to flee, but once more the nomads were quicker and managed to surround the fleeing rats again. Now they were pushing them back toward the burrow.

"Hold on!" Regus shouted. "They must not find the entrance to the nest."

He stood up as tall as he could and leaped toward the rat that he identified as the leader. It was a male, shorter than the others but of surprising agility. Regus tried to catch his breath as this rat circled him. From the corner of his eyes, he was still looking for Vasco, but he had disappeared. Where was he? Dead? Lost? Had he abandoned them?

In front of him, the enemy hissed and urinated in challenge. Then he jumped from side to side with such speed that Regus found it difficult to follow his movements. He no longer knew where his enemy was—in front, behind him, or by his side. By the time he understood what was happening, the nomad rat had landed on his back and was digging his claws in his nape. Regus cried out.

Immediately Coben came to his rescue. He threw himself at the aggressor with such viciousness that the enemy let go of Regus. Coben found himself stuck under the powerful body of his enemy, but he twisted his back in order to extricate himself and ran off.

"Not that way," Regus shouted after him, but he was too late—the panicked Coben entered the nest.

The nomad rat immediately sent out a rallying cry to his companions to show them the entrance to the burrow.

Regus froze. Nil! The little ones! Joun and the other females!

In a desperate leap, he rushed toward the second

entrance of the nest. Would he reach the main corridor in time to stop the nomad rats who were already gathering near the hole? He wasn't sure. As he skidded along the dark corridors, he couldn't stop thinking about Vasco. Why wasn't he coming to their aid? Where was he?

When he reached the main room of the burrow, Regus sniffed the scent of death. He stopped, his heart broken. The dull smell that permeated the air was coming from the corpses of rats. He had had so many occasions to smell the odor that he could not be wrong.

Overwhelmed, Regus advanced toward the nook where Nil and the little ones were sleeping. He looked for them with his whiskers and nostrils, and sent out a plaintive cry which was answered by Nil.

"We're here!" she said. "Lower!"

Regus' heart leaped in his chest. Alive! She was alive! But as he was about to join her, the ground started shaking under his paws. Clusters of dirt fell from the ceiling. The nomad rats were about to enter the main corridor!

"Stay hidden!" he whispered to Nil.

Then he darted into the corridor to meet the approaching enemy. He would never let them come near the females and young ones.

Alone in the dark, Regus listened. He could hear squeaks, rumbles, and the clattering of stones against the roots, which shook the walls of the corridor. Someone was coming, yet he did not pick up the scent of the nomad rats.

Puzzled, Regus crouched on the ground and waited.

Soon he sensed a presence nearby. He got up, ready to fight, ready to die, but then suddenly he recognized Vasco's familiar and reassuring smell.

"Regus?" Vasco called.

"Vasco!"

Happy to be still alive, the two rats squeaked, nosing themselves up against one another, mingling their whiskers.

"We were caught in a surprise attack," Regus said. "I waited for you. I looked for you! What happened?"

Vasco put his snout on the wounded nape of his companion and tried to appease him.

"I went to meet the nomads' chief. We came back just in time to save Coben. He was trying to defend the entrance to the nest all on his own. Where are Nil and Joun and the young ones?"

Regus did not really understand what had happened but he indicated the bottom of the burrow.

"They took refuge by digging farther down. I was going back up to help Coben and—"

He stopped, his body suddenly shaken with spasms. The memory of his fear was so intense that he kept shaking for several seconds more.

"You're hurt," Vasco said. "Come, let's get out of here. Then I'll return for the females."

When they emerged from the burrow, all the surviving males greeted them with squeaks of relief. Regus could see that Coben was among them. One of his ears was bleeding but he would survive.

Regus flinched when he noticed the group of nomad rats gathered around their chief. Bewildered, he turned to Vasco. How had he been able to negotiate with such barbarians?

"They're not barbarians," Vasco assured him. "Their chief's name is Kuok. He believes that we can learn to live on the same territory. Go and speak to him. He's waiting for you."

Regus limped toward the nomad rats. A few minutes ago, they were killing each other. But Vasco's intervention and negotiating skills had resulted in peace. Regus could hardly believe it. But as he neared Kuok, he discovered a chief who was surprisingly calm, and whose eyes shone with intelligence.

"If Vasco says so, then it must be possible," he muttered to himself.

22

The Last Battleground

When Vasco reached the bottom of the burrow, he detected a dull smell emanating from a corpse.

"Nil?" he called anxiously.

Right away, Nil came out of the dark, her swarm of little ones on her heels.

"What happened?" Vasco inquired. "Who got killed?"

Nil rubbed her fur against his coat. "No one was killed," she told him. "Come and see."

She guided Vasco to the corridor she had enlarged during the battle and stopped in front of a dark shape lying on the ground. Timidly Vasco drew near and sniffed at the cadaver. His throat tightened.

"Joun?" he whispered. "It's Joun. . . ."

Nil nodded. "She died suddenly."

Vasco crouched by the side of the old female, over-come with sadness. Joun was an integral part of his past and he would miss her terribly.

"I dug a hole for her," Nil continued.

She showed Vasco the hole that she had lined with moss and dried leaves. When he saw this burial nest, Vasco felt grateful. Joun deserved an exceptional farewell.

He grabbed the old rat by her ear with his teeth and dragged her body to the hole. Nil pushed aside the little ones who got in the way. Finally, Joun's body tipped to the bottom of the hole. The moss and leaves cushioned her fall.

Vasco raked a little dirt to cover the body, then looked at Nil. "We should go outside," he said. "We can't breathe in here!"

When they emerged from the burrow, Vasco observed that the entire tribe of nomad rats was present. The fe-males and young ones had settled near the brook and awaited the decision of their respective leaders. Among them, Zeya had a front-row seat, perched atop Tulai's golden coat.

Kuok moved away from his tribe and approached

Vasco, while Nil and her six little ones hurried to join Regus.

"Regus explained to me that he was not the chief of your tribe," Kuok said. "Did you lie to me once more?"

Vasco shook his head. Regus did not know it yet, but from now on he would be the leader. He just had to be told!

"I have no female, no little ones," Vasco pointed out. "My only family is Zeya, the blind female you kept as a hostage."

Kuok glanced kindly at his group of females. "Zeya is now a voluntary hostage," he said. "She's decided that she does not want to leave Tulai."

Vasco looked at Zeya and the pretty female with the golden fur. Zeya sensed everything. Now that Joun was dead, it seemed that Zeya possessed wisdom well beyond her years. She understood that by being adopted by both tribes, she would link them together.

Vasco and Kuok surveyed the battlefield in silence. Several males from both tribes were dead and others were wounded, but it seemed that an agreement had been reached. Vasco and his tribe would stay near the brook and hunt beyond the honeybee tree as much as they wanted. In exchange, Regus promised Kuok that he would teach him how to kill their common enemy—the gray snake with the deadly venom.

"We are nomads," Kuok added. "Soon we will move south."

He looked up and scrutinized the sky. "The rainy season is near. I advise you to dig another burrow, higher than this one. The one you have now will be flooded when the brook crests."

Vasco turned around and thought of Joun, buried at the bottom of the corridor. He could no longer sleep there anyway, so near to her body.

"We still have a lot to learn to live in the jungle," he said. "We will follow your advice."

He looked at Kuok again. This nomad rat had just confirmed that his dream had not been completely absurd. Two tribes, even when very different, could manage to cohabit on this earth.

"Thank you," he whispered.

23

Vasco, the Nomad

One morning, the jungle was silent. Not a cry from the monkeys, not a buzz from the bees. Nothing but the pounding of the rain on the leaves, ground, and animals. The rainy season had just begun.

In their new burrow, the tribe was busy protecting itself against the infiltrations of water. Openings were sealed with chewed leaves and mud, as advised by Kuok. Before the rain, the males had managed to stockpile the produce of their hunts. Nil was responsible for the distribution of the stock, but there was enough fruit, leaves, and spider larvae to feed them all for days to come. Regus accepted the status of chief, as suggested by Vasco.

It happened very simply, on the evening of the battle with the nomad rats. After each camp counted its dead and wounded, Vasco climbed over the roots of a monkey-bread tree that grew on the other side of the brook.

He looked at each rat, one by one. Among them he recognized those who had lived under Akar's rule and those from Olmo's tribe. There were also Tiel and Coben, who, like himself, had lost their entire tribe. And then there were Kuok's nomads. All of them, so different, were gathered here, ready to socialize and live side by side.

Vasco was moved and very tired.

"I accomplished my duty," he said to them all. "Now that the tribe has found a refuge, I can retire."

He stopped talking. The brook was singing between the rocks and moss. Perhaps Vasco was thinking about the long journey he had made since leaving his native harbor, and perhaps he was also remembering those who had fallen along the way, all those who had hoped with him and were no longer here to witness the fulfillment of their dream.

"It's not good to be the leader of a tribe for too long a time," Vasco went on. "You do not need me any longer. When things change, it is necessary to change the leader." He pointed to Regus. "Here is the one who will know how to guide you. He is a great hunter and a courageous and loyal rat."

He turned to Nil.

"And there is the one who will preserve our memory. Nil was here from the beginning. She shared our pain, our hopes, our fears, and our joys. Together Nil and Regus will be strong enough to decide what is best for the community."

Vasco came down from the roots of the tree and crossed the brook to join Zeya.

When she felt him near her, the blind female clung harder to Tulai's golden fur.

"I want to stay with Tulai!" she shouted.

"Very well," answered Vasco. "But did you ask Tulai's permission?"

The nomad female bowed her head and her whiskers quivered. It was her silent and calm way of showing her approval.

"But I want to stay with you too, Vasco!" Zeya went on.

In turn, he bowed his head. "I gave my word to Joun that I would look after you and I will keep my promise," he declared.

From that moment on, Tulai, Zeya, and Vasco were always together. For a while they alternated living in both tribes, going from the brook to the mossy rock. But in fact they spent most of their time in the high branches of the honeybee trees. They were a separate tribe of sorts, like a hyphen between the sky and the ground, between the past and the future. Vasco had never felt so free.

• • •

One rainy morning, Vasco came back to see his own tribe. He seemed at peace and determined. He took a tour of the new burrow, examined each corridor and nook, sniffing attentively, as if he wanted to take the smell of the nest away with him.

He approached Nil and Regus and rubbed his whiskers against the snouts of their little ones.

"I am leaving," he announced. "Zeya and I are going south with Kuok. Tulai wants to show me the salty marsh waters where she was born. It is a place near the sea."

His eyes shone with joy. He was going to be reunited with the familiar smells of the ocean, salt, and fish. He turned to Tiel and Coben, the only two survivors of the warehouse. He knew that they were adults now, fully capable of living their lives.

"We might come back in the dry season," he added. "If you're still here, I will come and visit you."

"We will be here," Nil answered. "This place is our home now."

Above their heads, the sky was darkening. Raindrops as large as bird eggs were falling on the leaves and ferns. Vasco ran to Tulai and Zeya, who were waiting beyond the brook. For the first time in a long while, he felt care-free and happy.

Nil and Regus huddled together to watch them leave. In spite of the rain, they were able to glimpse the golden shimmers of Tulai's coat as she and her companions grew smaller in the leaves.

"Vasco saved us and established a tribe that fulfilled his hopes," Regus said. "Now it is time for him to establish his own family."

About the Author

Anne-Laure Bondoux was born near Paris in 1971. She has written several novels for young people in varied genres and has received numerous literary prizes in her native France. Her previous novels published by Delacorte Press are *Life As It Comes*; *The Killer's Tears*, which was awarded France's prestigious Prix Sorcières and received a Mildred L. Batchelder Honor for an outstanding children's book originally published in a foreign language; and *The Destiny of Linus Hoppe* and its companion, *The Second Life of Linus Hoppe*.